www.penguin.co.uk

Also by Theresa Breslin:

GHOST SOLDIER
A thrilling, poignant story of hope and loss
set during the First World War.
'Another must-read novel by one of Scotland's finest writers' *Scotsman*

SPY FOR THE QUEEN OF SCOTS
A story full of secrets, betrayal and murder, set in sixteenth-century
France and Scotland.
'A gripping historical thriller from the brilliant Breslin'
The Bookseller

PRISONER OF THE INQUISITION
A gripping tale of fire, fury, love and revenge, set during the
Spanish Inquisition.
'Unputdownable' *The Times*

THE NOSTRADAMUS PROPHECY
A dramatic adventure story set in sixteenth-century France.
'Terrific novel . . . enormously enjoyable' *Guardian*

THE MEDICI SEAL
A gloriously rich and authentic story set around the life of
Leonardo da Vinci.
'A superb historical thriller . . . an enchanting novel about genius,
and a gift to an enquiring mind' *The Times*

REMEMBRANCE
An epic tale of young lives altered by the First World War.
'Immensely readable, passionately written' *Guardian*

SASKIA'S JOURNEY
A haunting tale of self-discovery.
'Mesmerising . . . truly memorable' *The Bookseller*

DIVIDED CITY
Two young rival football supporters are caught up in an attack on
an asylum seeker.
'A cracking good read . . . this is a book with far-reaching appeal
and universal themes that will encourage young readers to
challenge bigotry' *Guardian*

KEZZIE AT WAR
A spirited young girl fights to keep her family together.
'A remarkable story of hope and determination' *Val Bierman*

CAGED

THERESA BRESLIN

CORGI BOOKS

CORGI BOOKS

UK | USA | Canada | Ireland | Australia
India | New Zealand | South Africa

Corgi Books is part of the Penguin Random House group of companies
whose addresses can be found at global.penguinrandomhouse.com.

www.penguin.co.uk
www.puffin.co.uk
www.ladybird.co.uk

First published 2016

001

Text copyright © Theresa Breslin, 2016

Set in Goudy Old Style by Jouve (UK), Milton Keynes
Printed in Great Britain by Clays

A CIP catalogue record for this book is available from the British Library

ISBN: 978–0–552–56522–6

All correspondence to:
Corgi Books
Penguin Random House Children's
80 Strand, London WC2R 0RL

MIX
Paper from
responsible sources
FSC® C018179

Penguin Random House is committed
to a sustainable future for our business,
our readers and our planet. This book
is made from Forest Stewardship Council®
certified paper.

This book is for Carys Eloise

CHAPTER ONE

Blood.

In his mouth and on his tongue.

That last punch split his lip. Spinning him sideways to thud against the steel bars of the Cage. And he knew he'd taken a cut.

Blood has a stale taste. Brings back a memory. Don't think about that.

Move.

Fast.

Kai straightens. Beyond the Cage winks the red light of the camera. The fight would be on the Internet within hours. Would Evil Eddy be watching?

The blur of a fist. Kai dodges. Too slow. A whack to the side of his helmet leaves him dizzy.

Now Leo will come in to finish him off.

Gloves up.

But there's no one there.

Kai swings round. The Cage is empty. He shakes his head. Sweat pours from his hair down his face. Can't see. Pulls up his face visor to wipe his glove across his eyes.

Leaving his forehead exposed.

He hears the victory screech before he feels the impact. Leo drops from the roof bars onto his shoulders. Kai crashes to the floor of the Cage.

He is down . . .

. . . head battered onto the concrete.

. . . and out.

CHAPTER TWO

A splash of water on his face.

Spartacus stood over him. Seeing that Kai is awake, he emptied the whole bucket onto his head.

'Surprised at you,' he said, 'getting caught like that. And a bigger mistake was to pull up your visor.'

Kai scrambled to his feet. 'Won't do it again.'

Spartacus reached out and grabbed him by the front of his vest. 'You certainly won't!' He addressed the group of teens who were clustered outside the Cage. 'Listen up! All of you! No one, I repeat, *no one*, removes their face visor or helmet during a cage fight.' He glared at Kai. 'Got that?'

'Yes,' Kai mumbled.

'I can't hear you!'

'Yes,' Kai said loudly.

'It's not just about safety. It's to keep your identity a secret. The last thing we want is for anybody to find out who we are and where we live.'

The watchers growled in agreement.

Spartacus cupped his hand round Kai's cheek and said in a quieter voice, 'Get that cut seen to. Tech will have something suitable among his medical supplies, and let him do his concussion test routine on you.' Then he spoke to Leo, who was removing his visor and his helmet, shaped in the form of a lion's head. 'Well played,' he said.

Leo pulled off his gloves and raised his hand. Curling his fingers into a claw he let out a roar.

'Hey, Leo, turn this way and do that again.' Tech approached with the camcorder. 'It's a great shot to go in at the end of the fight.'

While Leo re-did his roaring lion act Kai climbed out of the Cage, took off his own gloves, visor and helmet and shoved them in his sports bag.

Stupid, stupid, stupid. He should have thought to look up. Where else could Leo have gone, apart from above him? What had distracted him? Kai fingered the tear in his lip. The taste of blood. That was it. Made his attention waver. Shocked a bad memory into his brain . . .

Kai thrust the thought away. It wouldn't happen again. *Fool me once – shame on you. Fool me twice – shame on me.* He was a quick learner. Although Leo was broader and heavier, Kai was faster and smarter – much smarter. And he'd proved it in their first fight of the tournament. Taken Leo down in two rounds, holding him to the floor until the end of the round so that Leo had to concede the match. People had thought Leo would win. He'd been tipped as favourite because of his build, screenshots of his naked muscled chest becoming an Internet hit.

Leo was beaming triumphantly as he was being filmed. Basking in the attention of the others, especially Boudicca, one of the three girl Cage Fighters. Clawing the air. Roaring to order.

'Don't do a close-up on the face,' Spartacus warned Tech as Leo stepped from the Cage.

'As if!' Tech gave him a withering look. 'It's his fingers I'm filming.' He laughed. 'Those nails will be a big attraction.'

Leo's admirers joined in the laughter. Leo had let his nails grow and filed them to look like claws. He now painted them a vivid orange colour for each fight.

Kai thought they looked ridiculous and took every opportunity to say so. He went forward and opened his mouth to speak.

'Shake hands.' Spartacus stepped between them.

'Of course.' Leo smiled. 'No hard feelings?' he said to Kai, holding out his hand.

'Course not.' Kai brought his fingers close to Leo's, avoiding actual contact with the orange talons.

Leo took his hand. 'Still mates?'

'Uh,' Kai muttered. They weren't mates, yet this was the way Leo behaved. Smooth and smiling when others were around – with the smile never reaching his eyes.

'You OK?' Raven asked anxiously as she came up.

'Fine,' both boys replied together.

Raven smiled at them.

'Catch you later.' Leo touched Raven lightly on the arm and moved away.

'You meant me?' Kai asked her. 'Right?'

'Of course I meant you,' said Raven. 'But I was concerned about Leo too. You landed some heavy punches on him.'

Kai glanced over his shoulder. Leo was staring after them. Raven turned and gave him a little wave. Leo waved back and grinned. But Kai had seen the look that was directed at him.

One of pure hatred.

CHAPTER THREE

Kai walked with Raven to Tech's den to watch him edit the film. She was as fast as Kai in the Cage and the favourite to win the girls' tournament. By the time they arrived there was an argument going on. Kai hung back at the door, not wanting to get involved.

'Leo cheated!' It was Sarema who was speaking.

Gita, her twin, nodded vigorously. Normally they were very quiet, but in an argument they always took Kai's side because he'd rescued them from an old skip down by the canal. Hiding there, Sarema had said, from relatives trying to arrange a forced marriage for them.

'Climbing up the bars to the roof of the Cage is cheating,' said Sarema. 'It was not a fair fight.'

She came and stood beside Kai. He glanced over at Raven, but she'd gone off to help Tech. They were hunting through his database and selecting more images to highlight the plight of street kids as a prelude to the movie of the actual fight. A slice of disappointment went through Kai. He'd half hoped Raven might be jealous of the attention he was getting from another girl.

There was a clamour of voices as people took sides.

'Cage fighting is a combo of boxing, wrestling and martial arts.' Boudicca was quick to defend Leo. 'So anything goes.'

'No way,' said Medusa, the third girl fighter. 'When Spartacus brought us together to be the *Cage Fighters for Freedom* we agreed there'd be no spitting or swearing, or biting, or gouging people's eyes.'

'Yeah, but we're not in any official organization,' said Beowulf. 'So Boudicca is right – we can do what we like.'

Boudicca nodded at Beowulf and he smiled, glad to have her approval.

'We're a completely independent group of fighters,' Boudicca went on. 'We make our own rules.'

'Which we did at our first evening Meet,' said Magog, a tall gentle-natured boy. 'As well as the things Medusa listed, there's no throat grabbing, and the referee's word is final.'

'Well, there you are,' said Beowulf. 'Spartacus acts as referee and judge. He awards the points for each round and decides what's allowed and he didn't call Leo out for cheating.'

Magog laughed. 'Spartacus would let anything go if he thought it would gain us Internet hits.'

'That's just what I said!' Boudicca made a face at Medusa. 'Anything goes!'

'It didn't in the first round, when I fought Raven,' said Medusa.

'Proper little lady, you were,' Boudicca said scornfully. 'Maybe that's why you lost!'

'But the boys did the same in their first round when they all fought each other,' said Medusa. 'They kept to what was agreed.'

'Well, I say we ramp it up for the final fights,' declared Boudicca. 'More excitement means more pay-per-views and our money goes up.'

'Dunno if we should change things,' Magog said doubtfully.

'Spartacus has already changed things,' said Beowulf. 'Leo and Kai came out with equal top points when we all fought each other, so he decided that they would have another two fights to see who'd be overall champion.'

'That was to do with how the tournament is organized,' said Medusa, 'not the actual fighting.'

'We can discuss it at the Meet later,' said Boudicca. 'But when it's our fight tonight you'd better watch out!' She made a pretend punch at Medusa. 'I'm going to put some new moves on you. Like what Leo did to Kai – which is why Kai lost, because he never realized what was going on. He didn't work out that Leo must have climbed the bars above him. Kai wasn't thinking fast enough. Where else could Leo be?'

'Maybe Kai thought Leo had left the Cage,' Magog suggested. 'The door isn't locked.'

'That's just daft,' Boudicca said firmly. 'Kai was too slow. Look! We can check it out on the film.'

Kai saw the big wall screen shimmer into life. The banner headline *Cage Fighters for Freedom* spiralled across it with a drum-roll announcement. Following this came genuine, un-staged footage of young people rummaging in waste bins behind fast-food outlets, an angled view of row upon row of spikes – mini-pyramids placed on a London underpass to deter homeless people making beds there – and a whole series of black-and-white photographs of teenagers and younger children living rough in the city. The voice-overs kicked in – street kids telling how they struggled to eat during the day and find a place to sleep at night. The *Cage Fighters for Freedom* banner returned along the top with screenshots of the seven fighters ranged below: masked, helmeted, and dressed in complete character costume.

The girls' photos zoomed to the front. Raven was in a full-length black dress with great glossy wings tremoring in hidden hues of lilac and purple. Snakes with flickering tongues coiled around Medusa's green silvered limbs, while Boudicca stood proudly in regal robes, crowned as the ancient warrior queen.

'We fight so the homeless will be heard,' Raven, Medusa and Boudicca chanted.

Then the boys' photos filled the screen. Leo, draped in

faux lionskin with claws extended. Magog, staff in hand and laurel leaves around his gladiator-style helmet. Beowulf wearing a plaid cloak, with metal bracelets cuffed on his wrists and upper arms. And Kai, in his trademark fiery red vest, poised for action within an ever-widening circle of flames.

'We fight for street kids to stay safe,' Kai, Leo, Beowulf and Magog chanted.

The screen dissolved and the seven photographs reassembled. Cage bars came crashing down to imprison them. A jagged bolt of lightning – and the bars burst asunder. Together, the seven fighters yelled their last statement.

'We are the *Cage Fighters for Freedom!*'

Their profile photos shifted to form a circle with the fight tournament information in the centre. After the first round of fights Kai and Leo were sitting equal at the top of the boys' table. Spartacus had awarded Leo more points than Kai for better performance and skill during the matches when they'd beaten Beowulf and Magog individually. But then, when they'd fought each other in the Cage, Kai had forced Leo into a submission which gave him a Technical Knock Out and brought their points level. They'd agreed to fight twice more for the championship.

On the girls' side, only one fight had taken place: Raven beating Medusa. Tonight Boudicca would fight Medusa, with the winner fighting Raven the following evening to decide who would be the girls' overall champion.

'Ladies and gentlemen!' Spartacus's voice, disguised by the megaphone he used, announced the midday game. The screen pixelled to another banner proclaiming Kai and Leo's second match. The letters slid vertically to halve the screen. On one side Kai's helmeted figure had a backdrop of flames ascending from an erupting volcano. On the other side Leo stood against film of a lion stalking its prey. Then Tech's edited version of the *Cage Fighters for Freedom*'s most recent fight was on the screen.

And the long and the short of it was that Kai *had* been too slow. It was clear where he'd faltered – exactly when he'd tasted blood from his cut lip, jolting him to recall the previous occasion he'd had blood in his mouth.

'What happened?' Raven spoke softly in his ear. She'd slipped through the group to be at his side.

Kai shrugged. One day he'd tell her, but not here, not now.

'What do you say, Kai?' Boudicca nudged his elbow. 'Was it a fair fight?'

'Yeah, do tell us what *you* think, Kai,' a voice spoke out. It was Leo asking the question. 'Isn't it true that you'd have done the exact same . . . if only you'd thought of it first?'

Kai gave a start. He hadn't noticed Leo come into Tech's den – but there he was, lounging against the far wall, his smile of triumph even wider than before.

All their eyes were now on him: Leo, Tech, the twins, and the other five Cage Fighters standing about in the disused Underground station they called home.

'What's true,' Kai replied, 'is that that I beat you in our first fight. You only won this second bout by playing a trick.'

'Not so much a trick, more like a neat move that you weren't expecting,' said Leo. 'You were too slow-witted to catch on.'

Kai, opening his mouth to reply, saw Sarema give a tiny shake of her head. She was right. He shouldn't rise to this bait. Leo was taunting him to make him say something he'd regret. He'd already lost to Leo in the Cage. He mustn't lose this battle of words too.

'It's a good get-out . . .' Kai paused so that his next sentence would have maximum effect. 'If you're scared of being beaten and want to run away from a fight.'

Leo flushed, an angry red stain spreading over his face and neck. He levered himself off the wall and strode across the room. 'I wasn't running away! Ever since I got here I've been told how clever you are, but this time I outsmarted you, you . . . Brainbox Boy!'

Kai drew in a breath as someone sniggered. The last thing he wanted was to have a babyish nickname like that stick. None of the street kids living underground used their real names. Either they thought of a new name for themselves or were given one by the group. He'd already chosen Kai, which meant 'fire'. He really didn't want to be labelled 'Brainbox Boy'.

'OK. OK.' Kai held up his hand. 'It was a neat move, Leo. And you won.' He spread his fingers. 'Peace?'

Leo ground his teeth, but with everyone there he'd no option but to acknowledge the gesture.

Their eyes locked in mutual dislike. Leo's gaze flitted to Raven. He forced his mouth into a strained smile. Then he bent his head and spoke to Kai as he pushed past him out of the door.

'Don't start what you can't finish.'

CHAPTER FOUR

After Tech had done the post-match medical check-ups, Kai went to his own den to get changed.

Despite having his helmet on during the fight, his head was now beginning to ache from the impact with the floor of the Cage. He massaged the back of his neck, then soaked a cloth in his wash-water barrel, wrung it out and pressed it to his forehead. A few deep breaths in and out and he felt better. He'd been close to losing his temper with Leo just then, but . . . better to wait until their final bout in the Cage. When he had that smarmy face in front of him he could smash it with his fist – make it a real Knock Out blow so there'd be no doubt about who was champion.

Kai looked down at his hands hanging loose by his sides. Spreading his fingers he examined his knuckles. Evil Eddy was always ready to use his knuckles . . .

Kai frowned. Abruptly he stripped off, slopped the

cloth across his body and towelled himself dry. He pulled on some clothes: bog-standard jeans, grey hoodie, black trainers. It was almost a uniform for the Cage Fighters. They didn't wear *any* bright clothing – as directed in the List of Rules.

Spartacus had drawn up a whole set of instructions which he'd printed out and pinned on their notice board.

The first three were:

> *Do nothing unusual.*
> *Do nothing out of the ordinary.*
> *Do nothing that attracts attention to yourself.*

The List of Rules was long, but the Cage Fighters obeyed them out of loyalty to Spartacus, who'd taken them off the city streets.

When Kai had first decided to run away from home, he'd headed for London. He'd known what the city was like, had scoped it out on the Internet before taking off. He wasn't dopey – his schoolwork was fine until the man he called Evil Eddy appeared in his house – so he made a plan. A classmate said his cousin would let him doss down in his flat, and he could find a job in one of the city markets. Once Kai was on the train he sent a text to his mum to tell her that he was with friends and not to worry. He sent her the same text every week and deleted her replies trying to persuade him to come home. He bought another cheap pay-as-you-go phone for everyday use and, although he missed her and his school friends, he was getting by and felt less stressed without Evil Eddy around.

Then one day his pal's cousin left with the rent well overdue, and Kai had to give the rest of his savings to the landlord's debt collectors, who threatened serious injury if he didn't pay up. He was reduced to sleeping rough wherever he could find a safe spot.

Kai hadn't expected the London streets to be made of gold, but neither had he expected them to be so dangerous. He thought that if he left folks alone they would do the same to him. But instead, as soon as it was apparent that he was homeless, he was pestered nonstop. There were shady people offering young boys as well as young girls 'free' food and accommodation. Creeps on the lookout for those who'd come to London with lots of hope in their hearts but little money in their pockets.

Eventually Kai made himself a squat by the river. He liked being near water and sometimes found useful objects which had been dumped from passing boats. But the market work soon dried up, which meant he was increasingly hungry by day and cold at night, and he and his clothes were getting scruffy. Then he began to be hounded by a gang who were operating on the same stretch of riverbank and twice had to fight his way free of them. He was on the point of packing his rucksack to move on when Spartacus had turned up. Said he was scouting for fighters and had heard Kai was handy with his fists. Invited Kai to talk over a project he was planning with similar teenagers on the streets. And so Kai met Magog, Beowulf, Boudicca, Medusa and . . . Raven.

Spartacus had explained his idea of staging a *Cage Fighters for Freedom* tournament in a steel-barred metal cage, and filming it for the Internet. Like the rest of the fighters, Kai was swayed by the plan to set up a pay-per-view website with a button where viewers could also donate to help homeless kids.

'Everyone involved gets a share of the pay-per-view cash,' said Spartacus. 'The donation money will go to a homeless charity. Some of you know Tech from the gym. The bank accounts will be in his name, and he's the IT expert who'll produce the films and manage the promotion side of it. If you guys get on board, then as well as giving you some income, it would raise awareness of how many young people are sleeping rough in Britain today. Public opinion might shame the government into doing something about it.' Spartacus stopped speaking and waited for their response.

It was an easy sell. Every fighter had their story of living in alleys or doorways, under a flyover or among a clutter of rubbish bins. Homeless creatures: half starved and jittery with fear of being beaten up, robbed, or worse.

Spartacus made his conditions clear from the start, the main one being that it was top-secret, as he didn't want anyone else muscling in on his project. He told them that he wasn't registering with any UK licensing authority. They'd regulate themselves, but they'd need to be hyper-careful as the police would definitely be unhappy if they found out that a group of teens were living in organized dens deep below street level.

Which was why the Cage Fighters respected Spartacus's rules. Everyone agreed that they felt secure here – especially as Tech had the entry and exit tunnels of their HQ monitored so no one could approach without him knowing.

Kai took his helmet and gloves from his rucksack.

Padded gloves.

In his heart he didn't like hitting people, but at least with gloves it was a cleaner way of doing it. Whereas using bare knuckles . . . he damped down the thoughts that were always there; ready to rise to the surface of his mind.

While Kai appreciated the gloves as being useful, his helmet he loved for the sheer glory of it. Tech was a wizard at construction. Not only with his electronics and electric wiring, but also at making things – the Cage Fighters' costumes were works of art. Kai's helmet was ebony black and decorated with an inferno of fierce red flames that seemed to leap and burn when he moved. Leo's had a background of jungle green with the bright orange head of a roaring lion.

Leo . . .

Something about Leo was niggling in Kai's head. An irritation, like an itch that needed to be scratched. There'd been animosity from the moment they met. And it wasn't just to do with the fact that Leo was Kai's main rival in the Cage. Although they were in competition with each other, the fighters got along OK. Kai knew that he was moody. Magog was annoying because he avoided his share of the chores. Medusa could be bossy and Raven short-tempered. Leo was sarcastic and Boudicca liked to argue – with Beowulf always pitching in on her side. But they painted each other's make-up and body tattoo-style art before their contests, played endless computer games, and all hung out together.

Except Kai and Leo.

Spartacus had noticed the tension between them as he introduced Leo to the group. 'Uh-oh!' he exclaimed when Kai reached out to shake Leo's hand. '*Powerful personality clash here!*'

Kai hesitated. Leo dropped his outstretched hand. And from that moment their relationship went downhill.

A big source of the friction was Raven. Beautiful, dark-haired, dark-eyed, mysterious Raven. She was fiercely independent, but Kai had been slowly building a friendship with her, and then Leo arrived on the scene. It was obvious that Leo liked her. The way he looked at Raven; the way he was always trying to chat to her riled Kai. When Kai had warned him off, Leo said he wasn't aware that he needed Kai's permission to be friends with Raven, and if Kai objected why didn't he speak to Raven about it? He'd smiled in his silky manner and walked away, leaving Kai fuming, because they both knew that Raven wouldn't be told what to do.

But Kai disliked Leo for more than that. He didn't fully trust him. The reason Leo had given for being homeless didn't seem right. Most of the Cage Fighters had good cause to be on the run. But they didn't share details of the what, or the why.

Only Leo, who came last to the group, had told everyone about his former life: wealthy, busy parents who didn't care about him, being sent away to boarding school where he was bullied, his retaliation where he'd broken the bully's arm, getting expelled, his failed attempt at suicide. Overhearing his parents talking with a doctor who'd advised a course of treatment involving a stay in a locked ward in a psychiatric hospital, Leo had done a runner, but lost his money and lived by begging on the street. Members of the group liked him for his openness, but there were bits of what he said that didn't quite fit together.

Kai promised himself that, one day, he'd investigate Leo's story and check if it was true.

And Leo was an expert at needling Kai. Constantly making sneering comments, trying to get Kai to lose his temper. Like in Tech's den, when Sarema had intervened. He'd need to thank her for calming him down.

Kai paused in the act of hanging up his helmet.

A thought jarred in his head. To do with Leo earlier. Not his taunting remarks. Something else . . .

Leo calling out. What was odd about that?

When Kai heard the argument going on, he hadn't wanted to go into Tech's den. He'd stood at the entrance while Raven went to the computer console. Sarema had come over to join Kai. Between them they blocked the door.

Yet Leo had called to him from across the other side of the room.

Tech's den was way bigger than anyone else's allocated space. It had been a connecting passage for Tube passengers transferring to another line. Tech had panelled the blocked-off end from roof to floor, making pigeon holes and dozens of nooks and crannies to keep his IT equipment. There was only one way in and out.

Leo was among the last to leave the fight arena. He'd been behind Kai and Raven as they were walking along the tunnel.

So, how had Leo got into Tech's den without passing them?

CHAPTER FIVE

All information must be shared.

That was another item on the List of Rules. Spartacus had explained that their very lives might depend upon it.

Outside his den, Kai slotted the door bar in place and went to study the map which Spartacus had fixed onto the wall next to the notice board.

Where Kai stood was marked as the Cage Fighters' HQ. A long time ago it had been known as Grove Road Tube Station, and was one of the earliest original London Underground stations. Grove Road, and the connecting tunnels surrounding it, had been closed down when the railway network was extended and redirected after the end of the Second World War. From here, different coloured lines radiated out showing these abandoned passages. Anyone finding a new one was meant to report to Spartacus so he could sound it out and add a coloured map. That way everyone would be kept

__own, yellow, black and orange lines meant they were OK to use. These were the huge old tunnels that had carried trains, plus a maze of other passages on various levels: air-vent ducts and those once used by maintenance workers, with connecting access shafts dotted here and there. The no-go ones were marked in bright red: the underground rivers, and the floodwater run-offs. When he looked at those lines Kai had to quell a rising sense of dread and apprehension. He shuddered. The bulk of the earth above, below and around, was a heavy, unyielding presence. Supposing there was a breach in one of the red-line passages? The force of the water could tear apart the ancient bricks and mortar. A torrent of foul water would come pouring in. Everyone would be trapped.

It was mainly Mole, a skinny, pasty-faced boy with a shock of dirty blond hair, who explored the unmarked tunnels. Raven had told Kai that the whole *Cage Fighters for Freedom* idea wouldn't have happened if Spartacus hadn't come across Mole, who'd spent most of his life underground. Mole wasn't interested in their plan to stage a Cage Fight tournament to draw attention to the number of homeless children in the city. He was working on a project of his own, and only agreed to help Spartacus find a suitable place for setting up his HQ in exchange for electrical equipment: torch batteries, cables and micro cameras to help him map unknown passages. From time to time he appeared with extra intel to add to the network on the map.

Some of the passages had names and numbers, and every Cage Fighter had memorized their own escape lines in case they ever had to leave in a hurry. In the event of an emergency Spartacus or Tech would press the alarm button and they'd evacuate immediately. Kai was with Raven on the northern exit. With his finger he traced their designated route.

North on Main Tunnel (green line) and down Access Chute Ladder 4 (blue); along to Air Duct 6 (brown); Air Duct 6 to Workers Tunnel 1 (white); Workers Tunnel 1 to Manhole Cover 9. Climb up and out to fresh air.

Fresh air.

Kai tilted his head back, closed his eyes and breathed in deeply. But the musty smell of the tunnels clogged his nose and mouth. He sighed.

'Time for tea?'

Kai opened his eyes and there was Sarema. She seemed to magic herself beside him whenever his mood was low or tense. He liked her company, and they walked together towards the café area. On first arriving in the tunnels, the Cage Fighters had worked with Spartacus to level out the rubble piled up in the gap between the old platforms. They'd laid down boards of wood to make a larger space for them to use and live in. At one end was the Arena which held the steel-barred Cage raised up on bricks, with training equipment nearby. The dens were scattered around: some at the bottom of the closed-off staircases, some hollowed out of the walls. In the middle was the place the Cage Fighters called 'the café', with kettle, microwave oven, a table and chairs. On the far side, near the toilet facilities, was the locked storeroom where Spartacus had stacked food and provisions. Beyond that was Spartacus's own den.

Gita was already sitting at a table in the café. She pointed to her cup and made a drinking motion. Kai nodded.

While Sarema was boiling the kettle, Kai thought again about how Leo could have got into Tech's den. On the wall map there was only a single line leading there. No new addition had been added as an entrance or an exit. Leo must have found another passage but wasn't sharing the information. Kai felt a glow of pleasure. Now he had something on that smug beggar. He'd save this for a suitable moment and then let Spartacus and the rest of the group know that Leo was breaking one of the Rules.

Sarema spooned herbs into a cup from a small hessian bag tied around her waist. The twins had taken to carrying food within the folds of their clothes – prepared to move on at short notice. Gita produced a snack bar from her sleeve, slid it across the table and pointed at it.

'Gita thinks you should eat,' Sarema explained.

Kai smiled his thanks. Gita ducked her head and

covered her face with her headscarf so that only her eyes were showing. Of the two girls she was the most traumatized by their experience of homelessness. She rarely spoke. It was left to Sarema, who was keen to speak better English anyway, to do the talking for both of them.

When Kai had found them in the skip, he sensed that it wasn't really the prospects of arranged marriages that had made them run away. From the little bits he'd learned about their former life, he guessed that they'd been trafficked into Britain with false promises of earning money in a legitimate job. Kai didn't hassle Sarema for more information as to what had happened to them when they reached Britain. He had secrets of his own that he wasn't sharing. He'd reckoned that if they didn't get something to eat and warm shelter soon then Gita might die. But it had taken an enormous amount of persuasion to get Spartacus to agree that the twins could come into the tunnels.

'We've been planning this project and laying down stores for weeks,' he'd said. 'We can't allow two stray girls to spoil it.'

'How could they spoil it?' Kai had argued back. 'They'll be happy to stay underground for a few weeks until the tournament is finished. When they've got their strength back they'll be in a better state to decide what to do.'

'How do you know there's not a full-scale search going on for them?'

Kai had thought of that. 'I dropped by an Internet café and checked some news sites.'

'I don't want any trouble from the people traffickers if they're looking for them,' said Spartacus. 'Those folks can be dangerous.'

'You took Raven, Medusa and Boudicca away from the sleazy scumbags that try to pick up young girls,' Kai had pointed out.

'I didn't rescue those girls because we're running a charity. I chose them because I thought they had the potential to be Cage Fighters. We have to keep focused on our main aim, which is staging the *Cage Fighters for Freedom* tournament. Our films show street kids fighting on behalf of street kids. Links to our posts are beginning to go viral on Twitter and key social media sites. And Tech's extra material will make our voice the one that shouts loudest about cuts to housing benefits, and every other anti-social policy that's made young people desperate and homeless.' Spartacus laughed. 'From your description of these two, it sounds as though they couldn't punch their way out of a paper bag. We don't have the resources for passengers.'

'Extra hands would be useful,' Kai argued. 'The fighters could do with more recovery and training time. We can't fight well if we've got to keep awake during the night watching the monitors. They could take our shifts and do some extra cleaning. You're always complaining about how messy this place is, how we'll be overrun with rats.'

Spartacus still wasn't for it. 'I'll give you one of the spare mobiles. You can go topside, make an anonymous call to Social Services saying where they are, and then throw the phone in the river.'

'They say they'll kill themselves if I do that.' Kai recalled the look on the girls' faces when he'd suggested calling the Social. 'And I believe them.'

'There are other organizations that can help, like the Samaritans. Ring them and let them take care of things.'

In the end, Kai threatened to quit if Spartacus didn't offer the twins shelter. Spartacus wasn't pleased, but had to comply. Amongst the Cage Fighters Kai was the most skilful and was racking up massive hits on the pay-per-view website that Tech had set up. With each bout the view numbers for the boys were increasing steadily. The girls – Raven, Medusa and Boudicca – had a solid fan base, and so did the other guys, but Kai's audience figures outranked them all.

Kai couldn't have abandoned the twins. They'd eaten most of the food they'd brought with them and were beginning to starve. Gita was shaking so much that she could hardly walk and it turned out that Sarema was useless at shoplifting. When he first met her, Kai had given Gita one of the snack bars he carried in case he ever got stranded. Now it was a special message between them. Gita always had a snack bar to give Kai.

Kai picked up the one she offered him. He tipped it to

his forehead to salute her. Ripping off the cellophane, he munched a chunk of it and exclaimed, 'Yum-eee!'

Gita giggled. Then a look of fright came into her eyes and she drew her shawl more tightly about her.

Spartacus dropped into a seat beside them. 'When Tech's finished the edit I'll go out and post the fight on the Internet,' he said.

'I know you check the view numbers when you're doing that,' said Kai, 'and give us feedback. But it's a pity we aren't able to watch the fights ourselves.'

'Do you think I'm exaggerating about you guys being so popular? I wouldn't lie to you,' Spartacus said gently.

'Of course not!'

'We can't have electronic communication going in and out of the tunnels. Tech's a genius at filching the electricity we use from various sources but it'd be too risky to use any Internet connection.'

'I get that,' said Kai, 'but it would be great for us to read the comments and find out how people are reacting.'

'I suppose' – Spartacus hesitated – 'someone could go out to gather intel on it. Their report would help motivate everyone for the final matches.'

'Are you saying that Kai may go up to the surface?' Sarema asked him.

Spartacus glanced at both girls, staring at Sarema for a moment longer before he turned and addressed Kai.

'You can go topside and do a recce on the fight. But you're not just going for a breath of air this time, so find somewhere you'll blend in. Maybe student accommodation or an Internet café.' He paused before adding, 'You can take Raven with you if she wants to go.'

'Thanks! Thanks so much!' Kai stood up so quickly that he almost knocked his chair over.

'Hold on.' Spartacus stopped him. 'Do you remember the rules for tunnel travelling and being outside?'

'I do.' Kai nodded eagerly. 'I'm always super careful when you let me go topside. I'll have my torch, follow the map lines and not draw attention to myself. Really, I will.'

'You'd better be,' Spartacus said half jokingly. 'We're almost there. This evening it's the girls: Medusa against Boudicca, then the winner fighting Raven tomorrow night. Beowulf and Magog have their third place play-off earlier tomorrow – at midday. Three matches, Kai, and then it's the build-up to the last match between you and Leo at noon on Saturday.' He grinned at Kai and fake-punched him on his shoulder. 'You'll not let Leo catch you out again, will you?'

'No way!'

Spartacus stood up and spoke more quietly. 'You need to keep your eye on Leo. He's slippery. Says one thing, means another. Never really know what he's plotting.'

'Yeah!' Kai agreed readily. 'I'll do that.'

Spartacus smiled as Kai hurried off to get his torch and find Raven.

CHAPTER SIX

The door to Raven's den was open and Kai could see her sitting cross-legged on the floor, braiding her hair. She glanced up as he approached and beckoned for him to come in.

Raven had the same furniture as all the rest: a bed, a bucket, and a metal box to keep possessions. That was it. But Kai and the others had personalized theirs. Stuck up posters and pictures from the pile of magazines kept in the café. Sarema and Gita's place was hung with an array of coloured scarves. Medusa and Beowulf even had family photographs pinned around. The walls of Raven's den were bare.

'Sure,' Raven replied when Kai asked her if she wanted to go topside with him on a special recce to watch the fight. 'There's something I want to buy anyway.'

Kai glanced out of the door. He could see Spartacus still standing beside the table in the café. He lowered his voice. 'You should ask Spartacus about that. Normally if we go out he doesn't like us doing anything other than walking about for a while or sitting in a park. This trip is for a special purpose.'

Raven flapped her hand in a dismissive gesture. 'He'd only tell me that totally everything is in the storeroom. That he spent weeks stocking up for this project. That it'll show how desperate homeless young people are and no one must do anything to jeopardize it. Yadda. Yadda. Yadda.'

Kai looked again in the direction of the café. He noticed that the twins had gone. They usually sat there in the afternoon and made tea and coffee for anyone who wanted it. Probably they'd left because of Spartacus. They knew Spartacus wasn't keen on them being in the tunnels, but was it more than that? Sarema *did* sometimes ask awkward questions.

'Hey, we're going to do well out of this,' Kai said to Raven. 'A few thousand pounds each, so we should stick to his List of Rules. And . . . he has been good to us.'

'Yeah, but I'm not going to be so grovelling grateful that I let him boss every aspect of my life,' said Raven.

'We get our cash the day after tomorrow, so I reckon it's worth doing what he says. What do you want that isn't in the storeroom? Spartacus has got everything anyone might need in there.'

'Apart from the special fluorescent wild-orange nail varnish Leo likes to wear,' said Raven. 'He borrowed it from me originally, but I only brought one bottle of that colour with me. And Leo's told me it's run out.'

'When did he tell you that?' asked Kai.

'We were chatting, and he mentioned that there wasn't much of the orange nail varnish left.' She wrapped the plait of hair around her head, fastened it with a clasp, and stood up. 'Let's go and get some more so he can pretty himself up for your last fight.'

'Did Leo come to your den?' Kai persisted.

Raven frowned. 'Why do you ask?'

'I was wondering when he asked you about the nail varnish.' Kai strove to keep his voice offhand. 'Did you visit him in his den, or—'

'Stop it!' Raven snapped. 'I'll talk to whoever I like, whenever I like.' She snatched up her hoodie and flounced out of the door.

'Sorry. Sorry.' Kai trailed after her as she marched angrily ahead of him towards the Main Tunnel, his thoughts tumbling over each other. Had Leo called by to speak to Raven? Or had *she* gone to *his* den?

He couldn't believe they'd met by chance. Leo never did anything by chance. All the rest of them had been recruited directly by Spartacus. But Leo had heard a rumour on the street that someone was seeking out young teenagers to take part in unofficial boxing matches. He'd asked around until he found Spartacus and approached him for a place.

'Spartacus stuck a note on the bulletin board saying

for us not to go near the old Langsdaine Station until further notice.' Raven slowed to let Kai catch her up. 'Been a roof fall in the tunnel leading to the bricked-up wall. And he said that when Sarema was on monitor duty she spotted some activity on Tech's camera outside the station. Workers clearing a birds' nest from the wall – which is fine – but that there was also a woman hanging about the closed-off entrance.'

'Police? Social worker?'

Raven shook her head. 'Dunno. From Sarema's description the person seemed more like a journo looking for a story.'

'Sounds like a spy. We've got time to scope it out before the fight goes up on the Internet.' Kai's spirits lifted. Obviously Raven had forgiven him for quizzing her earlier. She had a hair-trigger temper, but she didn't hold onto her anger for long. 'We can go north on the lines of our emergency exit, but branch off at the Workers Tunnel and come out at the manhole cover on the other side of the road in Langsdaine Park. It's a good place to watch the station entrance and we can see without being seen.'

''Cos it's near Bakerloo doesn't mean you're Sherlock Holmes,' Raven teased him. She turned on her torch as they entered the dim archway. 'I always hate this bit, when we leave our lit area.' She shivered. 'I'm not convinced that we're the only people down here.'

'We're not.' Kai spoke in a spooky voice. He stuck his own torch under his chin and switched it on. 'I'm a vampire!'

Raven feinted a punch at his face. Kai ducked his head and laughed. They walked on together.

As the darkness enfolded them Kai focused on a mental image of the map of the tunnels. For the first part of this journey they were following the path of their designated escape route. Their torches shed a brilliant light, but . . . supposing it was an emergency evacuation and he forgot his torch? Kai closed his eyes for a second. With no light to guide them, could he find his way?

North on Main Tunnel (green) and down Access Chute Ladder 4 (blue) . . .

Kai began to count his steps. He'd taken three hundred and twenty before he saw the blue blob of paint that Tech had painted on Access Chute 4. Kai shut his eyes. In complete darkness he wouldn't see that blue colour. He shone the torch onto the walls and the ceiling.

'What are you doing?' Raven was already squeezing into the access chute.

'Nothing much,' said Kai. He'd found what he wanted. Access Chute 4 was on the left-hand side of the tunnel. On the left-hand side of the chute opening, at shoulder height, a cragged piece of stone stood out from the wall. Kai put his hand on it.

'Come *on!*' Raven called to him.

Kai gripped the stone in his palm.

Memorizing the shape.

Placing a marker in his mind.

CHAPTER SEVEN

'Listen!'

Raven paused so that Kai caught up with her.

'Can you hear?' Raven asked him. 'The pulse of the city.'

Above their heads rumbled the never-ending London traffic.

'We're near the surface now,' said Kai. In his eagerness to be there he moved ahead of her onto the ladder leading up to the manhole cover. 'We could stay in the park for a bit before finding somewhere to watch the fight.'

It was springtime, but the clump of trees and bushes where the manhole was located were evergreen. And they were tangled together so thickly that Kai's head was concealed as he raised the cover and clambered out to the surface.

Through a gap he squinted up at the sky. Gun-metal

grey. It didn't matter to him that it wasn't the bright blue of a summer afternoon. He was happy with his feet on the earth and the vast vault of the sky above him.

None of the others bothered much about going up to ground level. The twins definitely didn't want to be on the streets. Sarema said that, after coming underground, it was the first time in weeks they'd been able to sleep properly. Before then, one would sleep while the other kept watch. And the rest of the Cage Fighters were prepared to focus on the training and put up with staying in the tunnels for a couple of months. But Kai hated the confined spaces and, anyway, he had less need of training sessions. He was much fitter than any of them.

He did feel safe underground, safer than he'd done for ages – no unexpected thump on his shoulder, no need to cower in fear of angry fists – but he missed the sight of the sky when he hadn't seen it for several days. Just being outside made him feel better. The background ache in his head receded. He breathed in to the very depth of his lungs, relaxing as the warmth of the air dispelled the dank smell that clung to his skin and hair. He smiled as he heard the faint burble and plash of water from the fountain in the park.

He'd be glad come Saturday when the fights were over. He should have enough money to pay for a rented room and food for a year. That's what Spartacus had reckoned.

'It will give you a clean start,' he'd said to the group. 'The rest is up to you.'

Kai was hoping to find a place on an island – somewhere surrounded by sea and sky. He offered his hand to help Raven climb out. Maybe she'd come with him. He'd wait to ask her.

Raven looked at Kai's outstretched hand and sniffed. 'I can manage on my own, thanks.' She swung herself up and landed on a pile of branches. They were careful not to move these or anything else there. On their previous expedition Kai had been tempted by a really good pair of trainers lying abandoned and apart, but Raven had advised him against taking them:

'Someone's hidden them there to come back later and collect them. Might be a shoplifter's stash. If they see that their loot's gone it'll make them investigate in this area. We don't want anybody discovering our tunnels.'

The trainers were still there, now placed neatly side by side among the roots of a tree. They walked through the park to find an empty seat. There was a tramp on a bench, sleeping. He was making noises, shaking and snorting.

Raven looked at him with pity. 'Bad enough his reality is a nightmare without having to fall asleep and have awful dreams too.'

Kai said nothing. He'd plenty of awful dreams of his own.

His eyes roved on. At the gates of the park a girl was feeding the birds. Setting out bread and then kneeling down to photograph them. Pretty. Long blonde hair scrunched up into a ponytail. She was making bird calls to bring them to her. Not that London pigeons needed any encouragement. There were dozens of them flocking in, greedily pecking at the crumbs. Opposite the park gates was the disused Langsdaine Underground Station.

Kai and Raven wandered around and came back to sit on a seat near the park gates where they could watch the bricked-up entrance. Kai draped his arm along the back of the bench. Should he wait a minute and then let it drop, casually, onto Raven's shoulder?

Raven shifted her position slightly. Kai hesitated. Had Raven moved closer to him or further away? He glanced around. Park gates – Bird Girl still cooing and clucking as she crept towards the birds. Old Underground station – all quiet.

Then.

A flicker of movement.

In the gap between two of the bricks – a blur of white. Kai pointed. 'Look!'

At the same moment Bird Girl stood up and fired off a dozen or so shots.

'She's the spy!' Raven yelped.

For Bird Girl's camera wasn't aimed at the birds. It was directed at a face peering out from the bricked-up Underground station.

CHAPTER EIGHT

'We need to get her camera!' Kai shouted.

Raven was already running.

So was the Bird Girl.

'Come back!' Raven cried out.

Bird Girl glanced over her shoulder. Saw them. Began to run faster.

In a fluster of wings and scattering leaves the birds rose, squawking, into the air.

Bird Girl was legging it like a maniac towards the street underpass.

Ignoring the blaring horns Kai and Raven crossed the street, dodging between the traffic. Instinctively they split up, heading for each side of the underpass. They were in the middle of the road when the sight of a blonde ponytail let them know she had exited the underpass. But they had her in a pincer movement! They reached the pavement. The girl was nowhere to be seen.

Raven signalled to Kai to look in the row of shops as they walked towards each other. Kai slowed down. Gulped some air. *Act unconcerned*. 'Pretend you're looking for a mate,' he told himself. It was a street of small shops, one or two of them mere kiosks. Nowhere for anybody to hide inside. Not if they were carrying a rucksack and a camera.

A camera.

What exactly had the girl photographed?

The blur of white. It was a face. Definitely. It was reeling through Kai's mind. But whose? Which member of the group would disobey Spartacus? It wasn't that they were frightened of him. It was more that they had all agreed to keep to his Rules. Most of them had a good reason for not wanting anyone to find out where they were. It was beyond stupid to do such a thing. And yet there was no mistaking what he'd seen. A human face at the disused station.

Kai popped his head round the shop doors. No sign of Bird Girl. He tensed as he got nearer the middle. Saw Raven hopping in and out of her line of shops. She wasn't having any luck either. They converged on the last shop. Went inside.

It was empty.

Bird Girl had disappeared.

Raven was frantic. 'We must find her! We must!'

Kai looked up and down the street.

'There was an Internet café on my side,' he said. 'A couple of people in it. She wasn't one of them.'

'Maybe she was hiding under a table?' said Raven.

They hurried back and looked in the window, scanning under the seats.

'She's not there!' Raven was distraught. Chewing her lips and grinding her teeth. 'If she's a journo she'll sell the story and it will be in the newspapers and then everything will be ruined. And me with it!'

Kai had never seen her like this. He reached out his arm to comfort her but she shook him off.

'You don't understand. If they trace me I'll be sent back to that vile hostel where I was living. The warden is a total creep. Seriously bad. He stalked me. And I don't have family to back me up. None whatsoever. So there was nothing I could do . . .'

'We've all got a lot to lose,' Kai said. He cast around in despair. Where could the girl have gone? He went over it in his head. He and Raven had fanned out on either side to capture her between them. There was no lane or alley leading off this street. The offices were secure entries. Bird Girl wouldn't have had time to punch in a key code and get inside. She *must* have ducked into a shop. But they'd checked each and every one.

Kai looked again at the Internet café.

'The toilets!'

They moved as one. Kai nodded at the young man on duty as they went past the desk. 'Buy a coffee in a minute. Need a pee.'

'Me too,' said Raven.

The gents' loo door was ajar. The ladies' had the engaged sign up. Raven put her shoulder against the lock and broke it open.

Bird Girl shrieked as Kai and Raven fell into the room, looking up in panic from where she was sitting on the toilet, laptop on her knees. The SD card from her camera was slotted into the machine.

'Stop her!' cried Raven.

Kai went for the laptop. But Bird Girl slammed the lid down.

'Too late,' she said.

'No,' Raven spat. 'Too late for you!'

The girl let out a cry of pain and fear as Raven grabbed her ponytail, winding it tight into her fist.

Kai stared in shock. Raven was wild. Beyond any normal fit of quick temper.

'She's ruined everything!' Raven howled.

Laptop clattering to the floor, Bird Girl stood up, turning round, trying to get free. Raven kicked viciously at her legs to make her fall on her knees. She wrenched Bird Girl's head back, exposing her neck. A gleam of steel – and a knife appeared in Raven's other hand.

'Jeez!' Kai gasped. He took a step forward.

'Don't come near!' Raven hissed. 'I'll slash her throat if you do.'

CHAPTER NINE

There was a single second of silence in the room.

Bird Girl spoke first. 'What d'you want?' she whispered.

'Shut your face!' Raven brought the knife up to Bird Girl's eyes. 'See this? I've used it before. I'll take your tongue out if you speak again.'

'Raven,' Kai said desperately. 'We gotta think this through.'

He could see that Raven was tipping over the edge. Her hand was trembling, her mouth and eyes twitching.

'Jam that door shut,' Raven ordered him. 'Don't want any witnesses.'

Kai backed up against the door. His mind was racing, trying to work out how best to calm Raven down.

'The café might have CCTV; so might the street.' Kai talked in a soft tone of voice, aware of the dumb appeal in Bird Girl's terrified gaze. 'If something bad happens here then our cover is blown and we never go free. We need to think what Spartacus would say, what he'd do if he was here.'

The mention of Spartacus had an effect on Raven, for she acknowledged that Spartacus was a person who'd helped her. The knife was unsteady in her hand.

'I reckon we should find out where those photos were sent,' Kai suggested.

Raven jerked her head in a half-nod of agreement.

Kai looked at Bird Girl, and asked the question Spartacus had asked every Cage Fighter. 'What's your story?'

'My little sister is missing.' Bird Girl was shaking so much she could hardly get the words out. 'I've been trying to find her. Following clues. I think she's being kept prisoner behind the closed-up wall of the old Langsdaine Underground Station.'

'We don't keep people against their will,' retorted Raven. 'None of the Cage Fighters would—'

'Shhh!' Kai shot her a warning glance. In her stressed state Raven was saying too much. 'Where did you send the photos you took? To a newspaper?'

Bird Girl shook her head. 'My Cloud,' she said.

'Give us the password then,' said Raven. 'We're gonna delete them.'

'Please.' Bird Girl began to cry. It was a piteous sort of sobbing. 'Please, please don't delete the photos. They're the only lead I have of where she might be. Nobody else cares about her any more. Not the police, nor Social Services. I've got to get in there and search for her.'

Kai and Raven exchanged glances.

'Your little sister isn't in that tunnel,' Raven said shortly, 'and that's a fact.'

'How can you know for sure?'

'We just do,' said Kai.

'Is that your squat? Do you live—'

'It's us that asking the questions,' said Raven. 'Not you.'

'If you know where that tunnel leads I'd pay you to take me there.' Bird Girl spoke quickly. 'How much do you want? I've got money on me. Not much, but I could go to the ATM.'

Someone rattled the handle of the toilet door.

'We can't stay here,' Kai said.

'We can't let her go,' said Raven.

'We could contact Spartacus,' said Kai. 'He might be OK with us letting her go if she promises not to publicize this or say anything about what she's found out.'

'I don't trust her.'

'What other option do we have?'

'This.' Raven swiped the air with her knife.

'Don't be daft, Raven. We wouldn't get far on the streets before we were caught. And where would we go? We couldn't go back to the dens in case we left a trail to the others. We'd be held for days and interrogated nonstop. They're allowed to do that now. You can only hold off the police for so long, and if the newspapers get wind of this then we're done for. Our secret would be out *and* we'd betray Spartacus too.'

The word 'betray' made Raven falter. She brought the knife close to the girl's eyes. 'Is that a deal? We let you go and you say nothing to no one?'

Bird Girl looked at the knife in Raven's hand then looked at Kai. To Kai's amazement she slowly shook her head.

'No,' she said. 'I'll only promise to keep quiet if you take me with you so I can look underground for my sister. Otherwise you can kill me right now.'

'You don't know what you've got yourself into here,' Kai said.

'No, I don't,' Bird Girl replied. 'But what I do know is that I don't care what you guys are up to. All I'm interested in is finding my sister. If you're familiar with the tunnels then maybe you could help me do that.'

There was a rap on the toilet door and a voice said, 'Whatever's going on in there, can you finish up quick-like, 'cos I got an urgent need.'

'We haven't decided how this is gonna play out yet,' said Kai, 'but we'd better move somewhere else, that's for sure.' He picked up Bird Girl's rucksack and shoved the laptop and camera inside.

Raven slipped the knife into her sleeve and Kai realized that she must have always carried it there. She saw his glance and gave him a defiant look. 'Don't look at me like that. I wasn't strong enough to complain about the hostel warden. I was on my own and it was the only protection I had.'

Pulling up the hood of his top Kai shouldered the rucksack and opened the toilet door. 'Sorry, mate,' he said to the girl who was hopping from foot to foot outside.

Raven pushed Bird Girl ahead of her and they left the café. 'Where are we going?' she asked Kai as they got into the street.

'It's Spartacus's decision whether she's allowed into the group. One of us has to stay with her, while the other one goes back and asks him what we've to do.'

'Where can we take her so that she doesn't make a run for it while that's happening?'

'I won't run off,' said Bird Girl.

'No one said you could speak!' Raven stamped her boot on the girl's foot.

Bird Girl grimaced in pain but she didn't make a noise.

'I know a place we can keep her,' said Kai. 'It's where Sarema and Gita were hiding out before they joined us. We can walk there. In a line,' he added, 'with her between us.'

'You lead the way,' said Raven. 'I'll go last.' As they got into position Raven leaned over Bird Girl's shoulder. 'Remember I've got my knife,' she said. 'You try to run and I'll bury the blade in your back.'

CHAPTER TEN

The abandoned skip where Kai had found Sarema and her twin was in amongst a pile of rubble and tree branches, and far enough away from the canal towpath not to be noticed by any passer-by. Kai dragged a long thin plank from where he'd hidden it under some bushes and placed it up against the side.

'This is how Sarema and Gita got in and out,' he explained. 'There's a slide on the other side. When the twins were living here they'd pull this plank up after them so no one could follow and they'd be safe. You go first.' Kai indicated for Bird Girl to climb the plank.

'May I have my rucksack?' She held out her hand. 'Please?'

'No way!' Raven waved her knife menacingly. 'Do as you're told and get on with it!'

Bird Girl walked slowly towards the plank.

Kai spoke to Raven in a low voice. 'I'll stay with her

while you go and tell Spartacus what's happened. Avoid Langsdaine Park in case anyone in the area of the park or the old Langsdaine Tube station noticed the kerfuffle earlier and is snooping about. Maybe try the school entrance. You'll get picked up on one of Tech's monitors. Give the "help" signal and whoever is on monitor duty will let Spartacus know and he'll send someone up to meet you.'

Raven gave a watery smile. She never went in the tunnels unless someone was with her.

'Breathe deep, breathe slow,' said Kai, 'and you'll be fine.'

To his surprise Raven gave him quick hug. 'Thanks.'

She'd spoken so fast that Kai wasn't sure if she'd actually said it. He decided to believe that she had. But she'd definitely hugged him. And that was a big step for her. In their previous lives, the Cage Fighters had been through tough times which made them suspicious and mistrustful of others. Of all of them, Raven was the most wary. It had taken Kai weeks to establish their friendship and for her to tell him that she'd been in trouble with the police and run away from whatever place she'd been sent to live. Spartacus was the only person who knew every individual's history. He didn't ban them from sharing their stories, but he didn't encourage it either. 'Look to the future,' was one of his sayings. 'We've all got a past we'd like to forget.'

Kai felt privileged that Raven had shared more of her

past with him. He watched her negotiate the barbed wire that fenced off the towpath and begin to run towards the main road. When he turned round, Bird Girl had stopped and was crouched on the plank.

'Hurry up!' Kai raised his voice. 'You're almost above the trees there. We don't want anyone catching sight of you.'

Bird Girl didn't move. 'How do I know that you're not going to tip me in there, pull the plank away and leave me to die?'

'Why would I do that?' said Kai. He came to stand underneath Bird Girl. Her eyes were grey, the grey of a stormy sky. They showed fear, but also determination. He saw then that she wouldn't go quietly into the skip. He'd sent Raven away too early. He should have kept her – and her knife – here, until Bird Girl was inside.

They stared at each other. He realized she'd deliberately not gone far up the plank. She'd been waiting until he was alone because she was thinking about jumping to the ground. She'd probably been working out her escape while he was talking to Raven. Estimating the height from the plank to the ground and the terrain she'd have to cover in order to outrun him to get to the fence, over it, and onto the path.

The trees were beginning to bud but were quite bare, so from where she was positioned she would see that the path was empty. Beyond that was rough wasteland and then more trees. In the distance was a common where folk exercised their dogs.

But that was much further away. The dog walkers didn't venture here. In the weeks during which Kai had visited this area he'd never met anyone. The nearby water wasn't a main canal. It was a side channel, probably used years ago for coal barges to tie up. There was no one around to help Bird Girl, even if she screamed – and he could see that it was dawning on her that he was taller and stronger, and would catch her.

He watched her shoulders sag at the hopelessness of her situation. She glanced at the top rim of the skip. And, in a moment of clarity, he saw the scene from her point of view and appreciated her fear. Once she was in there she was trapped. Kai understood then that, despite the odds, Bird Girl was going to try to make the run.

She looked at Kai. 'Uh, OK.' She smiled. 'I guess going inside the skip is the best option for me.'

Kai smiled back at her, pretending he believed her. But he was a fighter. Could sense a feint before it happened. And earlier, he'd been fooled by Leo in the Cage. He wasn't about to let it happen again. He prepped up, ready to grab her and bring her down. Just as she tensed herself to spring off the plank there came, carried on the wind, the distant sound of children somewhere. They were calling to each other in whatever game they were playing. Bird Girl raised her head, hearing it the same moment Kai did.

And Kai suddenly knew what to say. 'Take a minute to think about your situation,' he said. 'You're desperate to find your little sister. You think she's in the old tunnels of the London Underground. If you alert the police it'll take you ages to convince them. By the time they arrive she could have disappeared. You might never reach her. You know by now that me and Raven can take you into the tunnels. We are the best chance you have of finding her.'

Kai held Bird Girl's gaze. She was listening to him.

'If we were going to murder you I'd have kept Raven, and her knife, here with me. And' – he tapped the rucksack – 'I've got your camera and laptop.'

Bird Girl looked at the rucksack and bit her lip.

Kai was fumbling in the dark, but he might have found a chink in her armour. He took the rucksack from his shoulder and held it out. 'Here,' he said. 'It's yours.'

Bird Girl stretched down and took the rucksack from him. Still she hesitated. 'Are you following me into this skip?'

'Yes,' said Kai. 'I can't wait out here in the open.'

'How do I know I can trust you?'

'You don't,' he said. 'It's a risk you have to take.' He unzipped his hoodie and opened it wide so that she could see there were no inside pockets. 'I don't carry a knife.'

Bird Girl nodded. 'OK.' Placing her hands on each side of the plank, she began to crawl towards the top.

CHAPTER ELEVEN

Kai saw Bird Girl look down into the skip. She glanced back at him in surprise and then disappeared over the edge.

Kai ran to the top of the plank and heaved it up behind him. He joined Bird Girl where she was standing at the foot of the slide he'd set up to take him safely down to the bottom of the skip. Sarema and Gita had used the same plank of wood for outside and inside the skip, but what no one knew was that after they'd left, Kai had gone back to the skip. Outside he'd piled up earth, chunks of masonry and heaps of branches to conceal it and then made himself a second 'home'.

He'd installed a plastic chute from a kid's outdoor play unit that he'd found in a dump. To drain off rainwater he'd attached an angled pipe to it which went through a hole in the bottom of the skip. Inside the skip Kai had built a rough shelter, dry and vermin-free. Plenty of spiders, but no mice or rats as far as he could tell. He'd set traps for them and they were empty. Any food he had he kept in tins. The roof of his shelter was sound and it too had a gutter leading to his drain. It would be his bolthole after the Cage Fighters' project was finished. Give him somewhere to hide out while he made his plans. By that time he would have enough cash to travel to one of the islands he wanted to visit, find a cheap caravan let, and get by on casual work.

'Is this where you live?' Bird Girl asked, pointing to the small wooden hut that took up half the floor space of the skip.

Kai didn't reply. He was beginning to regret coming here, but he hadn't been able to think of anything else. They'd needed somewhere to go and Raven had looked as if she'd use her knife at any moment. He opened the hut door and gestured to Bird Girl to go in.

'Oh!' she gasped. 'Oh, it's lovely.' She turned to look at Kai. 'Did you do the decoration?'

Again Kai didn't answer.

The walls of the hut were covered with myriad magazine and newspaper photographs.

'The beach in Bali,' said Bird Girl, reaching out to touch one. 'It's beautiful. Have you been there?'

Kai shook his head.

She examined the rest of the images, reading out the names as she went:

'Zanzibar, Madagascar, Goa, Skye, Sark . . . Oh, I see! They're all islands.'

He definitely shouldn't have brought her here. She was too observant. Now she was trampling through the private parts of his soul.

Bird Girl's brow furrowed in a way that should have made her unattractive, but didn't. 'Oh,' she said softly. 'This is your personal stuff.' She stopped looking around and sat down cross-legged on the floor. 'I'm sorry if I was being intrusive.'

'It's OK.' Kai affected not to be bothered. It was a strategy he'd learned. Don't let people know the things you cared about. If they knew, then they had power over you. They could use it to punish you or make you sad or angry.

Like Evil Eddy used to do.

'Oh, *sorry*,' Eddy would say in a syrupy voice as he picked up one of Kai's childhood models and bent a piece. 'I seem to have damaged your itsy-bitsy toys.'

Kai had long since given up model-making but his mum had arranged some of his more complicated constructions along his bedroom windowsill. 'They're not toys,' Kai had shouted in rage and frustration. 'They're *models*.'

'Models? Models!' Eddy had repeated what Kai said, adopting a sing-song voice as though speaking to a baby. 'Are you referring to your itsy-bitsy cutesy model *toys*?' And he'd keep goading him until Kai's temper flared into violence and he'd rush at Eddy, arms flailing, his feet kicking at his shins. Eddy would laugh and hold him at arm's length until Kai was exhausted, on the verge of crying. Then Eddy would pick him up and dump him on his bed and say, 'Time for itsy-bitsy baby boy to have a nap.' And march off, whistling.

When Kai's mother came home from work Eddy would show her the bruises and scratches on his arms and ankles. 'I was trying to help Kai with his homework when he got in from school. But he was fooling about with his models and then he broke one and tried to blame me. Went berserk, so he did. Lost his temper.'

'We need to talk about this.' Kai's mum had tried to make peace between them.

Kai refused to speak, but Eddy chatted away while he served dinner. 'Typical teenage behaviour.' He winked at Kai's mum. 'Don't you worry about it, love. Kai and I will sort it out eventually.' He gave Kai a hard calculating stare. 'Won't we?'

Kai bolted his food and went to his room. Later his mum came to speak to him.

'Did you kick Eddy?'

'Mum, I—'

'He's got a bruise the size of a football on his leg.'

'But he started it—'

Her eyes went round with horror. 'You mean Eddy kicked you?'

'No. I didn't mean that.'

'Has Eddy ever hit you?'

Kai shook his head. 'No.'

At the time that had been true. To begin with, Eddy's way of bullying involved play-act wrestling games where he yanked Kai's arm up his back and gave him sly nips and skin twists. But when Kai tried to explain this, his mum patted his hand.

'Eddy told me he's trying to toughen you up,' she said. 'He thinks that because we've been on our own together for so long you've been too sheltered. That as you grow older, you might not be able to cope with the big bad world.' She paused. 'Kai, could you make an effort to get on with him? When your dad died I never thought I'd find anyone else. Eddy says he loves me and wants to take care of us.'

'Do you love *him*?'

His mum blinked several times before replying. 'Uh-huh,' she said. 'I think I do.'

After his mum had gone Kai lay back on his bed. Slow tears gathered behind his eyelids. He hadn't dared ask his mother the next question that was in his head: *Do you love him more than me?*

Kai came back to himself, aware that Bird Girl was crying – a strange muffled sound that frightened him more than if she'd begun screaming.

'Thank you,' she sobbed, 'for . . . earlier. I thought your friend was going to stab me. I was petrified.'

'So was I,' said Kai.

Bird Girl gave a nervous laugh.

Kai laughed too then, and the tension between them lessened.

'It's mad that I'm laughing,' said Bird Girl. 'It's not funny.'

'Raven has . . . issues,' said Kai. 'Whatever happened in her past has made her very jumpy. I don't know everything about her 'cos we all keep ourselves to ourselves.'

'Sounds as though there are more than two of you?'

'Uh.' Kai gave a noncommittal response. He'd need to be more watchful. This girl was plenty smart.

'Look,' said Bird Girl, wiping her face on her sleeve. 'I don't know what's going down with you guys. And I don't want to know. You probably think I'm a journalist after a feature, or a private detective. I'm neither of those things. Truly I'm not.'

Kai held up his hand. 'Best save your story for when Spartacus arrives.'

'Who is Spartacus?'

'He's just . . . Spartacus.'

'I'll be honest with you,' Bird Girl went on. 'I'm scared you've called on some thug to beat me up.'

Kai laughed out loud at the thought of Spartacus deliberately hurting someone. It wasn't in his nature, and anyway Spartacus was a small man who walked with a limp. The bones of one leg had been shattered when he was fighting with the army in the Middle East, and his condition made worse by post-traumatic stress disorder. He was intensely bitter about the way society treated disabled soldiers after discharge. He'd bitten the head off Tech when he'd mentioned Help for Heroes. 'I don't want charity! Ex-soldiers shouldn't have to rely on *charity* if they're injured when doing their duty and serving their country!' Then he'd clammed up and refused to discuss it any more.

'Spartacus couldn't beat anybody up,' said Kai. 'When he was in the army he had an accident which left him lame in one leg.'

'So he won't come into the skip?' she asked.

'Nope,' said Kai. 'And although he's a straight-talking guy, he won't harm you either. I see why you might not trust me, but—'

'Actually,' Bird Girl cut in, 'I do trust you.'

The words hung in the air. In the fading light from the open door her eyes had changed to a deeper shade of grey.

Kai's breath caught in his throat. He steadied himself. 'But then, you really *have* to trust me, don't you? The question is; do I trust you?'

They had to wait until early evening before Kai heard someone calling his name outside the skip.

Raven had returned.

CHAPTER TWELVE

Within a minute Kai and Bird Girl were outside.

Dressed in a long coat, Spartacus was standing behind Raven. His head was covered with a floppy cap concealing his hair and crammed down over his forehead. Dark glasses shaded his eyes and a thick scarf muffled his neck and chin.

He disregarded Bird Girl and spoke to Kai. 'This is a mess!' he said. 'A total mess!'

'What else could we do?' Kai asked. 'There was someone behind the bricked-up Underground station and she . . . Bird Girl, took a photograph of whoever it was.'

'I put a note on the bulletin board saying to avoid the tunnel near Langsdaine.' Spartacus's voice was strained with suppressed anger.

'We did,' Raven chipped in, 'but you didn't say anything about the park opposite.'

Spartacus scowled at her.

'It's just as well we went there, because if that photo goes public then we're finished.' Kai walked forward to give Spartacus the rucksack. 'We had to take Bird Girl's camera and laptop so we could check it out.'

Spartacus searched inside the rucksack. 'Camera, notebook, laptop . . .' He listed the items as he found them. He looked at Kai and Raven. 'Where's her phone?'

'Her phone!' Raven let out a squeal. 'Kai, we forgot about her mobile!'

Kai's stomach spasmed. In the confusion of trying to control Raven he'd not thought of Bird Girl's mobile. One of Spartacus's biggest rules was *no mobile phones*. At all. Ever. He'd taken the Cage Fighters' phones and locked them in the safe inside the storeroom.

Spartacus clicked his fingers at Bird Girl. 'Give me your phone,' he ordered.

Bird Girl hesitated. 'I don't have a—'

'Yes you do,' said Spartacus. 'Please hand it over without a fuss.'

Bird Girl fumbled a phone from inside her shirt.

Duh! Kai struck his fist to his forehead. What an idiot he was! He should have realized she would have a phone.

Spartacus took the phone. 'She's sound-recorded something recently!'

A sense of betrayal swept through Kai. He turned to Bird Girl. 'You were recording what I was saying?'

She blushed. 'Look at it from my side,' she said. There

was a plea in her voice. 'I'm kidnapped off the street. Threatened to be stabbed with a knife, and—'

'A knife!' Spartacus broke in. He addressed Raven. 'You swore that you wouldn't ever carry again.'

Raven dropped her head. 'I feel safer. You know why.'

'Yeah, I know why. I also know that, for you, carrying a knife is an offence in itself. If you were stopped and searched that would be enough to have you sent back. Do you hear me?' Spartacus raised his voice. '*Sent back*, Raven. Back where you came from!'

Raven hunched her shoulders and began kicking at a clod of earth.

'Someone might hear us.' Kai plucked at Spartacus's sleeve. 'This place isn't so very far from the main canal path.'

Spartacus waved Bird Girl's phone in Kai's face. 'She's got the emergency services on speed dial!'

Kai's heart flipped. Behind him he heard Raven give a strangled sob.

'But I didn't use it.' To Kai's surprise Bird Girl stepped right up beside him and spoke quickly. 'I did not phone the police.' She paused. 'I could have. I had an opportunity to call the police, but I didn't.'

'That must be true,' said Kai. 'We'd be surrounded by blue lights by now if she'd done that.'

'Two nights!' Spartacus was quieter but still angry. 'Only two nights to go,' he repeated, 'and we'd be in the clear.'

'I'll stay with you guys for two nights or longer,' Bird Girl offered. 'Then you'll have a guarantee that I can't tell anyone whatever it is you're doing.'

'Someone will miss you. Someone will report that you've disappeared,' said Kai.

Bird Girl shook her head. 'No they won't. I'm a photography student and I've got my own place. I'll text my college friends and tell them I'll be away and out of contact for a bit.'

'That might work,' Kai said to Spartacus.

'It would. Definitely,' Bird Girl agreed. 'It will be you that sends the text,' she added, 'and sees the replies.'

'Not from here then,' said Kai. 'Let's do it from somewhere else so that it's picked up on a different phone mast.'

'Where is "here", exactly?' Spartacus glanced at the skip and then at Kai.

'Just somewhere I thought of that would get her off the street and wouldn't compromise what we're doing,' said Kai. His breath began to quicken. He didn't want Spartacus becoming too interested in the skip. It was his private place which he'd discovered by chance. He'd been sitting on the opposite bank watching the water one afternoon when he'd seen Sarema and Gita climbing out via the plank which they had then shoved under some bushes. He'd followed them about the city and saw how they shopped in different areas of London. Always in big supermarkets and wearing scarves to hide their faces, they bought the cheapest of food.

He'd thought the skip as a den was a terrific idea. At first he hadn't disturbed them. It was theirs and he wasn't going to frighten them off. When he'd checked up on them in a few days he'd noticed only one girl, Sarema, going in and out; the amount of food she was bringing back was becoming smaller and smaller. He guessed their money was almost gone and the girl didn't look street-wise enough to be any good at shoplifting. Kai crept closer. When he heard the other girl coughing he knew they needed help.

He left food along the towpath – a carton of sandwiches, a bag with pastries – trying to make it look as if someone had let them fall accidentally. But then the sick girl's cough got worse and he realized they must leave the skip before she became seriously ill.

Once Kai had forced Spartacus to take the girls underground he still had to persuade them that it would be dryer and warmer there, and explain about Tech and his box of medical supplies. Kai contrived a meeting with Sarema on the towpath. He told her that it was he who was leaving food for her to find, and made her realize how bad her situation was.

When Sarema finally brought Gita to meet Spartacus in an empty lock-up, you could see that the girls were scared witless. But Spartacus had Raven with him, and underneath the twitchy aggression Raven could be kindly. She spoke to the twins and explained about the *Cage Fighters for Freedom* project. How there were seven street kids – three girls and four boys – who were fighting each other in a special tournament to raise money for the young homeless and put pressure on the government to increase youth welfare programmes. The fights were being posted on the Internet – plus information to show that, with no jobs and no affordable accommodation available, young people were caged for life. Spartacus was their leader and Tech an IT expert who'd set up a pay-per-view website where each fighter would earn a percentage of the takings.

With the Cage Fighters dressed in their character costumes and the polished steel bars of the Cage glowing in the single spotlight, it was an instant Internet hit. Through the training fights and the qualifying bouts of the tournament they'd built a dedicated fan base. Now, in the lead-up to the finals, their online audience was growing even larger. Raven persuaded Sarema and Gita to come underground and abandon the skip.

Except the skip hadn't been abandoned. For when Kai had gone back to collect the twins' belongings he'd made it into this secret den of his own. A place he wanted no one else to know about . . .

Spartacus moved past Kai and went closer to the skip. 'This'll be where the twins were living when you rescued them.' He tapped the rusty metal. 'It'll be filthy with vermin by now?'

Kai nodded, not trusting himself to speak the lie.

'It's full of crap!' said Bird Girl.

Kai started at the interruption.

She wrinkled her nose. 'I don't know what your tunnels are like,' she said, 'but they have to be better than that.'

Spartacus swung round. 'You don't talk until I say you can!' he rasped. 'I need time to think about this. Raven told me you had some story of a missing sister. I want the details before agreeing to you being with us. Not at this moment,' he said as Bird Girl began to speak. 'We'll go somewhere else.'

'Where?' asked Kai.

'The Rail Depot. You guys go on ahead and I'll follow.'

CHAPTER THIRTEEN

The Rail Depot wasn't actually a rail depot. It was a basement lock-up near a train station. It wasn't a tunnel access either – Kai expected Spartacus to treat Bird Girl the same way as the twins and not take her anywhere near the tunnels before she'd told him her story. This empty lock-up was where Spartacus had interviewed Sarema and Gita before allowing them to join the Cage Fighters. Bird Girl would have to convince him that she was trustworthy before he'd let her underground to live with them.

Spartacus put on a dull overhead light. The lock-up was small enough for Kai to see that it was no longer empty. Boxes were now stacked in one corner.

'Equipment for Mole,' Spartacus said quickly as he noticed Kai looking at them. 'Tools and such-like. That lad always wants to dig deeper and deeper. I do believe he's daft enough to think he'll reach the centre of the Earth. But I've got to keep him sweet so that he'll let us stay in his tunnels until we finish the tournament.'

So what Raven had said was true, thought Kai. It was Mole who'd shown Spartacus the tunnels he'd discovered, not the other way around.

Spartacus took out Bird Girl's phone. 'From the point when you were chased from the park did you call or text anyone at any time?'

Slowly Bird Girl shook her head.

'Why not?' And as she didn't answer Spartacus said, 'Are you stupid? Or crazy? Or both?'

Bird Girl flushed. 'I'm not stupid. Possibly a bit crazy. Worry can do that to people, you know.'

'Oh, I do know that,' said Spartacus. He moved closer so that his face was only centimetres from hers. 'What's making you crazy, Bird Girl? Eh? Tell me why you allowed yourself to be kidnapped off the street by people you've never met before, managed to keep your phone hidden from them, had the opportunity to use it, and yet you did *not* dial the emergency services.'

Bird Girl moved so that her feet were apart. Without backing away from Spartacus she replied steadily, 'Because I want to find my sister. She's the most important thing in my life.'

'Why do you think your sister is in the closed-off Langsdaine Underground Station?'

Bird Girl sighed. 'It's hard to explain.'

'Then we need to hear your story,' said Spartacus.

'There's no "story" as such. I had this very strong feeling that's where my sister was. Now' – she gestured at her rucksack – 'I think I've got proof that I'm right. Please, *please* can you help me?'

'Your story?' Spartacus repeated.

Kai felt a flash of pity for Bird Girl. She was being evasive and that wouldn't work with Spartacus. Kai recalled when he'd told Spartacus his own story. Spartacus had locked eyes with him, his gaze boring into the depths of Kai's soul. Unnerved, Kai had glossed over the events that had caused him to run away, masking unpleasant things with half-truths and outright lies. But it only took a few brisk questions from Spartacus before Kai was blurting out stuff about Evil Eddy, stuff he'd vowed never to think about again.

Bird Girl was scared, that was obvious, but her voice was firm as she began to speak.

'My name is Maxine—'

'No. It isn't,' said Spartacus. 'Stop right there. We never use our real names.' He glanced at Kai. 'I thought she'd agreed on being Bird Girl?'

'Not exactly.' Kai squirmed at Spartacus's irritation. 'I thought of that name for her because of the way she was calling to the birds when we first saw her in the park.'

Spartacus switched his gaze back to the girl. 'You get to choose your own name. Let me know when you decide, ASAP.'

'I like being "Bird Girl" – I'll stick with that name.' She gave Kai a tiny smile. 'Thanks,' she said.

A fizz of pleasure shot through Kai and he smiled in return. From the corner of his eye he saw Raven pout.

'So,' Spartacus addressed the girl in a kinder tone, 'you are Bird Girl. We all have pseudonyms so that no one knows who anyone else is.'

Apart from you, Kai thought suddenly. Spartacus knew everyone's identity and probably every secret they owned and wished to keep hidden. But no one knew Spartacus's real name.

'It makes it safer for us,' Spartacus went on by way of explanation.

'Uh. OK,' said Bird Girl. 'I can see the sense in that. And I guess "Bird Girl" suits me.'

Spartacus nodded encouragingly. 'Tell us why that name is so appropriate.'

'I was genuinely taking photos of the birds in the park.' Bird Girl pulled something from her pocket. It was a long bird's feather. 'This feather is from the wing of a goose. Look!' She held it to her lips and blew so that it ruffled. 'It's a genius of design,' she said. 'In the spring and autumn, when they migrate, Darcey and I used to watch them fly across the sky. We always said that, one day, we'd go with them.'

'Darcey?'

'Darcey, my little sister. That's why I'm here. Darcey went missing and—'

'We need a name for Darcey,' Raven said brusquely. 'Even though she's not here. If you're speaking about her, then you have to give her a new name.'

'OK,' Bird Girl thought for a second. 'Let's call her "Dove".'

'That's a lovely name for your sister.' Spartacus moved away from Bird Girl to give her more space. 'Why don't you tell us about her?' he suggested in a soft voice.

Kai saw Bird Girl's own stance relax, and the atmosphere of hostile suspicion in the room lessened – and it struck him how adeptly Spartacus had managed that.

Bird Girl took a deep breath. 'A couple of days ago my little sister . . .' She paused. '*Dove* went out and didn't come back. Dove is . . . different; she doesn't see the world the way we do. And so, even though she wrote me a note to say she was going away and I'd not to worry about her as it wouldn't be for long, I *am* worried, very worried. I – I—' Bird Girl broke off, tears shining in her eyes.

'Go on,' Spartacus prompted.

'I've always cared for her since she was a baby.' Bird Girl hesitated. 'My mother was vulnerable. She was a drug addict and my dad kept her supplied, but when he saw she was becoming a problem – needing more and more – he moved on. One day he was there and next day he was gone. My mother's mental health issues became worse, and when she found she was pregnant, she had a breakdown. But she wanted to keep the baby. She seemed to cling onto this as the only reason for her existence.' Bird Girl made a wry face. 'It wasn't for me that she wanted to stay alive. I didn't seem to matter to her any more.'

A silken thread of understanding spun from Kai towards Bird Girl. He was familiar with that sensation. Of not being enough for a parent. Not being quite what they wanted, not being able to give them what they needed to keep going.

'Anyway, the baby was born and it became apparent that she had special needs. My mother couldn't cope. Within a few years she was dead. And so it was just me and Darcey.' Bird Girl hesitated over the word. 'Sorry, I mean "Dove". We were put in a children's home and shunted between a whole series of foster families. But as we grew up there weren't so many fostering opportunities.'

'No offers of adoption?' asked Spartacus.

Bird Girl twisted her mouth. 'One or two, but only for me.' She lifted her head and said defensively, 'Well, I'm blonde and bright, aren't I? I was a very pretty little girl. Dress me in frilly pink and I'd smile and sing a song or recite a poem. I could say and do all the right things to attract adopting parents. But Dove, well, she hadn't a clue about trying to please. Had to be reminded to wipe her nose.'

'You never *were* adopted though, were you?' said Spartacus.

'No, because I refused to be adopted unless my sister

was too. But Dove struggles to keep her attention on what's happening around her. She has this habit of focusing her mind intently on a particular thing. People get cross with her when she doesn't answer them. They think she's deliberately being rude, but shouting won't bring her out of it. I was the best person at coaxing her back to reality. So I wasn't going off with a new family and leaving her to fend for herself at the children's home. Some of those places aren't nice.'

'Too right!' The words burst from Raven's mouth.

'Quiet!' Spartacus spoke gruffly.

'OK, OK,' Raven replied. She shuffled her feet and moved into the shadows.

'Last Christmas, when Dove turned sixteen, they set us up to live together in a supported flat. I was always interested in photography and enrolled in a college course. I'm even beginning to make some money out of my photos. With that and our allowances, we manage. I'd walk her to and from the centre she attends and we were fine until spring arrived and we had our usual argument. That's when she decided to take off.'

'If she's sixteen and left you a note then the police won't be chasing around looking for her,' commented Spartacus.

'They checked with our previous foster carers and other places we'd stayed,' said Bird Girl. 'And they said they'd keep a lookout, especially at train stations and anywhere we'd been on holiday, but it's not a high priority. Now that she's older my sister is quite able to feed and dress herself and generally get by in the community. And she'd taken money with her.'

'What's the argument you always have in the spring?' Kai asked.

'My little sister becomes restless as spring approaches. When she hears the cackling of the migrating geese she starts to nag me about going after them. It's because that's what I told her we'd do – from when we were young and were taken into care. I promised her that, one day, we'd get on a secret train and follow the geese wherever they were going. Every spring she'd say, "Can we leave now?" and every spring we'd have a row when I said we'd need to wait until we were old enough to leave the children's home. This year, as soon as she spotted the geese going over, she rushed to pack her bag. She thought that because we weren't in the home any more we could do it. As the days passed she became more agitated, saying that if we didn't get on the secret train right away we'd never catch up with the geese.' Bird Girl looked sorrowfully at the feather she still held in her hand. 'I kept putting her off. One night we had a massive argument. The next morning her bed was empty.'

'I still don't understand why you thought she might be in the closed-off Langsdaine Underground Station,' said Spartacus.

'Each day on the way to her centre we walk past Langsdaine. A couple of weeks ago she picked up some feathers and told me she'd seen a bird flying in through a crack in the wall. I said it had probably found a good nesting place. Every time we passed she'd stop and stare at the wall. She was worried that the bird had got trapped inside, and needed rescue. I looked about but there was no way in or out that I could see. She said maybe it was a magic bird and it had been leading us to the secret train that we could get on to follow the geese. I tried to talk her out of this idea. But she became more and more convinced that there was something going on behind the bricks. She has acutely sensitive hearing. She was saying strange things. That there were people behind the wall. She could hear them moving about and talking. Said there was a hidden camera too.'

Kai and Raven exchanged a startled glance. Spartacus's face remained impassive. 'Did you investigate further?'

'No,' said Bird Girl. 'She was becoming fixated on this so I began to take another route to her centre. She stopped talking about it and went back to nagging me about following the geese.'

'Did you tell the police any of this?' Spartacus's voice was casual as he asked the question.

'Some of it,' said Bird Girl. 'I told them about the birds' nest. I didn't say anything about Dove hearing voices. I didn't want them to think she was disturbed enough to be put in a locked unit if they found her. My sister isn't dangerous, but people are prejudiced against those who are different.'

'Too right,' Raven said again – murmuring so that it was only Kai who heard her. And as Spartacus indicated for Bird Girl to continue speaking Kai saw Raven slide her knife back inside her sleeve.

'They got Tube maintenance workers to examine the wall,' Bird Girl went on. 'And there was a birds' nest in a recess high up, but they said that the whole wall was solid and double-thick. Not even an infant could squeeze through.'

'Yet you persevered in thinking that's where your sister was?'

'It was all I had. I thought she might come back there to try and find the secret train, so I decided to hang out in the park and photograph the birds while watching the entrance. And then . . . the one day I think I may have seen something, you guys grab my camera and – and—' Bird Girl crouched down on the floor and put her head in her hands.

There was a long silence in the room.

Spartacus took off his sunglasses. He spoke very slowly and distinctly. 'On the condition that you do exactly as I say and you never tell anyone what you see or hear, I will take you underground and try to find out if there is a way into the old Langsdaine Station from the inside. But!' He held up his hand as Bird Girl began to thank him. 'You must stay with us for two more nights – that's tonight – Thursday – and then Friday night, right through until late Saturday evening. And before we go underground, you will need to write texts we can send to your friends to let them know you're away for the rest of the week.'

'I could say I've gone to look around in Brighton,' said Bird Girl. 'My sister and I were often taken there on holiday. I've already mentioned that idea to my friends and the Social Work support staff.'

'OK.' Spartacus pulled out her phone and handed it to Raven. 'Tell Raven what to say and who to text. We're involved in a charity project which is neither criminal nor a security threat, but for the moment it needs to remain secret. You must not break our trust or try to escape before then. Do you understand me?'

'Yes,' Bird Girl replied. 'I will not try to escape.'

'I'm warning you that we'd know if you did. We'd be on to you before you got ten metres. There's a camera on every exit from our headquarters.'

Kai knew that the tunnels leading to their HQ were monitored. But he'd always thought of it as being for the protection of the Cage Fighters, so that no one could get in without Spartacus knowing. Now Kai realized that it worked both ways – neither could anyone get out without Spartacus knowing about it.

CHAPTER FOURTEEN

On leaving the lock-up, Raven made a face behind Bird Girl's back as she walked ahead of them.

A stab of sadness pierced Kai and he wondered why. He'd always wanted Raven to like him so much that she'd be annoyed with any other girl he spoke to – but now that it was happening, he was uncomfortable.

Before they were near the school entrance to the tunnels, Raven left them, heading for Victoria Station. Spartacus, who was neurotic about security, wanted the outgoing texts to go through the mobile masts in the area where the trains left for Brighton.

'You never know,' he explained to them. 'The police might call Bird Girl and then track her phone use if she doesn't respond. If they follow it up, then the signal coming from Victoria Station fits in with the message we've agreed for her to put in her texts.'

After sending the texts Raven would switch off the phone and return to HQ.

'I'll take your phone out again at some point tomorrow,' Spartacus told Bird Girl. 'That way I can scan your incoming messages in case any need a reply.'

'You could say I'd forgotten my charger,' suggested Bird Girl. 'Then they wouldn't be bothered if they don't hear from me for a while.'

'I'll decide what's best to be said.'

Spartacus's voice had an edge on it and Kai sensed he was deeply distressed at the turn of events.

In the boiler room of the boarded-up school Spartacus tied his scarf around Bird Girl's eyes. 'You keep this on until I say otherwise. We're going underground.'

Bird Girl shuddered. And before Kai thought about it too much he reached out and touched her hand. Her skin was damp with cold sweat.

'It's an easy entrance,' Kai reassured her. 'Sixty steps down a ladder and then a long descent to walk, not too steep.'

'OK. Thanks.' Her voice was thin and she clenched her teeth together.

Kai guessed it was Spartacus's favourite exit and entrance because it was such a simple way in and out. But he wasn't surprised when Spartacus made unnecessary turns, doubling back several times. He'd done this with the twins too. Obviously it was a ploy to confuse the newcomers so they weren't sure where the Cage Fighters' HQ was located. But whereas the twins had gone along in a trance-like state, Bird Girl groped around her, feeling the walls. Kai's torch was bright enough to illuminate the way ahead and he was able to see if there were any loose stones or debris lying in their path. But, in addition to those times when he warned her to be careful, Bird Girl often stopped, especially when they were changing direction. And, as they continued through the tunnels, Kai began to think that it wasn't because she was wearing the blindfold that Bird Girl was acting this way. She was trying to memorize the route in her head.

Sarema and Gita were standing in the café when they eventually trailed into HQ. The twins must have been keeping a lookout on the monitors for their arrival. Pots of tea and coffee were on the table and they'd made sandwiches.

'Food. And drink.' Sarema pointed to the mugs and plates.

'That's great, Sarema.' Kai suddenly felt immensely tired and hungry.

Spartacus didn't thank the twins. 'Good that you're about,' he said. 'Saves me having to call on you.' He unwound his scarf from Bird Girl's eyes. 'This is Bird Girl. She's your new roommate.'

'But—' Kai opened his mouth to object. The twins' living space was so cramped that there was hardly enough room for them.

'Yes. Of course,' Sarema said. She held out her hand to Bird Girl. 'Welcome.'

Bird Girl grasped Sarema's hand as if she would never let it go. 'Thank you,' she managed to say. 'Thank you. Thank you.'

Sarema took Bird Girl's hand between both of hers and rubbed it. 'Cold,' she said. 'You are frozen. Time for tea?'

'Bird Girl needs to be made aware of everything we're doing here,' said Spartacus. He was clearly irritated at how Sarema seemed to have taken charge of the situation.

'But food first.' Kai sided with Sarema. Avoiding eye contact with Spartacus he sat down on the nearest chair.

Grudgingly Spartacus sat down too.

Bird Girl let go of Sarema's hand. Her body started to tremble, her legs gave way and she flopped onto a chair. Kai pushed a plate towards her. 'Try to eat,' he said. 'You'll feel better if you have food in your stomach.'

Overwhelmed, Bird Girl covered her face with her hands and began to cry. The dry sobbing tore at Kai's heart. He leaned across to pat her shoulder but Spartacus pushed his hand away. 'Best leave her alone,' he advised, then sat staring into space until Bird Girl recovered herself. 'I want to speak to a couple of people,' he said. 'I'll be back shortly.' He motioned for them to eat.

They ate in silence until Spartacus returned. He spoke first to the twins. 'Please fully explain the *Cage Fighters for Freedom* project to Bird Girl. From now on she is under your care. Show her the List of Rules. Make her understand how crucial it is that everyone obeys my orders for the next couple of days. If either of you, or' – he glanced at Kai – 'you, meet any of the Cage Fighters, tell them that I'll update the whole group at the nightly Meet which will take place after Medusa and Boudicca's fight.' He lifted Bird Girl's rucksack. 'I'm going to lock this in the storeroom until Tech can check it out.'

'Can't we do something now?' Bird Girl asked. 'Is there a tunnel from here that goes to Langsdaine Park?'

'No.' Spartacus shook his head. 'But I will find a way through there as soon as I can. Try to relax and trust us' – he indicated Kai – 'to do the right thing.'

Bird Girl looked beseechingly at Kai. He gave a half-nod and shifted his gaze. What Spartacus had said wasn't strictly true. There *was* a way to reach the tunnel which led to Langsdaine Park. Maybe Spartacus didn't want to alarm Bird Girl by telling her that the roof was collapsing.

'Raven should be back soon,' Spartacus went on. 'Beowulf is on monitor duty. When he spots her on the way in he'll tell Leo to go and meet her.'

'I could do that,' said Kai.

'I've just spoken to both of them to arrange it. With Raven still topside, Tech will need your help to film tonight's fight between Medusa and Boudicca. You go to his den now and give him a hand to prepare his equipment.' Spartacus stood up. 'I'll walk with you.'

Before they reached Tech's den Spartacus drew Kai aside. 'Don't go back to that skip,' he said. 'Not ever.'

'I won't,' said Kai.

'It will tempt you.' Spartacus spoke earnestly. 'From what Sarema and Gita told me they'd made it into a cosy nest with shawls as curtains. Yeah?'

'It was OK.' Kai nodded. 'But I gathered up their gear and brought it here for them.' He didn't add that he'd replaced the girls' shawls with postcards and photos cut from magazines, and made the shelter inside the skip wind- and waterproof.

'It's served as a safe place on two occasions so it's going to be oh so tempting for you to return. Don't do it.' He looked at Kai expectantly, as if waiting for him to agree.

Kai said nothing.

'This is good advice I'm giving you.'

Kai shrugged. 'Whatever you say.'

Spartacus gripped Kai by the shoulders. 'I'm talking about afterwards. When we've got the money and had the share-out. You'll think it will be OK to go there and hide out before moving on. I'm telling you not to do it. The police aren't incompetent. They've got high-end tracking devices, plus it's their job, so they can do that slow, dogged detective work where they pick up clues and follow leads. When this breaks it'll have a big media hook. Amateur detectives will play super-sleuths, physically, but mainly on the Internet, hunting on Twitter and social networks. These guys have enough savvy to co-ordinate calls from mobile phone masts.'

'You've got our mobiles,' said Kai. 'When I get mine back I won't even switch it on.'

'That's what you say now. But you'll want to check missed calls and texts. Or you might trust someone who blabs without meaning to. And when you leave the tunnels you'll yearn to go somewhere familiar. When you're living rough a place like that calls to you. You lie at night not sleeping and you think about it. What you might add to it to make it a home for yourself . . .' Spartacus's voice tailed off.

Kai didn't want the skip as a home. The Cage Fighters were to split up after the last fight, telling no one where they intended to go. It would be safer that way. When he received his very final pay-out Kai planned to head for an island off Wales, where his dad had come from. It was why he'd chosen his name: 'Kai' – like the Welsh dragon, breathing fire. But he'd need a place to stay until then, and if everyone else was on the move at the same time then he'd be safer lying low for a while. So, on the days he'd been allowed to go topside he'd started to prepare, taking some of his personal stuff to the skip, including his original phone – the one he used to text his mum.

But Spartacus was right. The skip had served as a safe haven on two occasions. To use it three times might be a mistake. It was like being in an army tank with one entry, one exit. If he got caught in there he was done for.

Kai shivered as he went into Tech's den.

CHAPTER FIFTEEN

Beowulf lifted his head briefly from the monitors as Kai came in. He was on the lookout for Raven as he knew she didn't like being in the tunnels on her own and he was keen to spot her as soon as she was underground.

'You OK?' Tech asked Kai.

'Raven and I had to bring someone in. We'd no option,' he added quickly.

'I heard,' said Tech. 'When Raven came back without you Spartacus was still topside posting your fight with Leo. While she was waiting for him to return she told me what went down in Langsdaine Park.'

Kai looked at Tech. He wondered if Raven had mentioned the knife. They shared an interest in film and she worked with him to sift through his database of digital images to choose the best ones for the publicity material. But Tech was a few years older than the Cage Fighters and quite reserved. He didn't often mix with them socially.

Usually he was immersed in his work – like now. Even as he spoke to Kai his fingers were whizzing over the keyboard.

'I'm improving the fighters' profiles,' Tech explained. 'I'll update Boudicca's and Medusa's on the footage that goes out with tonight's fight.'

He clicked the mouse and the big screen filled with overlapping frames of Boudicca in character mode, the focus homing in on her golden gloves and then the golden crown on her helmet. Tech had animated the crown so that, with a glorious burst of sound, it spun in rapid movement. A shower of sparks whirled outwards, filling the screen with a kaleidoscope of colour.

'And I've given Medusa more serpents than the Reptile House at London Zoo,' Tech boasted. To the slow beat of a snare drum the camera delved into a roiling pit of tangled snakes – asps and adders, hooded cobras, pythons and venomous vipers, and rattlesnakes coiled to strike. Cymbals crashed and a deadly black mamba reared up from the centre of the pile. Mouth agape and fangs forward, the slitted yellow eyes sought their prey . . . and then the camera zoomed out to reveal the eye slots of Medusa's face visor and the swirling snakes on her neck torque.

'Impressive,' Kai told Tech. 'Your Cage Fighter name should be "King of the Keyboard".'

More clicks brought images of Kai onto the screen. 'Nearly finished your file, Kai,' said Tech. 'By the time I'm done your name will mean more than "fire". You'll be the "Firestorm Fighter".'

The noise of a rushing wind swept into the room – followed by the fearsome crackling of a forest fire raging out of control. Tongues of flame licked up, devouring the screen and morphing into the flames on Kai's vest, until the shot panned back revealing Kai punching his way through the inferno.

'Wow!' exclaimed Kai. 'I'll buy that!'

Tech seemed pleased at Kai's reaction as he closed down the computer, but his face was serious as he said, 'Spartacus is none too happy about us acquiring another passenger with only a couple of days to go before the pay-off.' His remark was a statement rather than a question.

'Yeah,' Kai responded. 'But I don't think we should worry too much. This girl – Bird Girl – has promised she'll stick to our rules and do what we say until after the fight on Saturday. Spartacus says he'll update everyone later on at the Meet. He sent me here to help you get ready to film tonight's fight.'

'I'm always ready.' Tech patted his satchel. 'Just hanging until I see Raven coming back in.'

'There she is!' Beowulf jumped to his feet. 'I'll let Leo know so that he can go and meet her.'

Kai's mind seethed with resentment as he went with Tech to the Arena. Here he was, stuck with Tech, who probably didn't need any assistance, while Leo was off to be with Raven.

*

When they reached the Arena Spartacus was chatting to Boudicca. Medusa was already in the Cage.

Medusa in action was like the snakes which adorned her from hips to helmet. Her body was slim and sinewy and her fight method was more akin to wrestling than boxing.

Boudicca climbed in beside her. She had cast herself in the role of the ancient British queen whose name she'd chosen. She stood erect and threatened Medusa with an imaginary spear.

Because they didn't have a live audience, Tech used CGI to make a crowd and added in sound effects of applause, catcalls, yipping, barking and whistling. Through the megaphone the voice of Spartacus rasped out the announcements.

'Ladies and gentlemen! I present . . .' He paused for a moment, knowing that at the edit stage Tech would insert a trumpet fanfare. 'The hideous snake-infested Gorgon – Medusa! Look not upon her face, for one glimpse of her eyes will freeze your blood for ever!'

Tech moved in with the camera as Medusa lay down and slithered on her stomach towards the bars of the Cage.

'And,' Spartacus went on, 'fighting Medusa in this match is: Boudicca! Queen of the Iceni, who sacked London and subdued the Legions of the Roman Empire!'

'Instead of wearing that old balaclava Spartacus should

dress like a Master Gladiator when he's refereeing,' Kai said to Tech. 'It would ramp up his introduction.'

'Absolutely no-go on that one,' said Tech. 'I'm never to film him. He made me swear to it. He's neurotic about being recognized.'

'Pity. You could have made him a terrific executioner-style helmet as disguise.'

'Yeah, but nothing would conceal his bad leg.' Tech switched off the camera as Spartacus limped over.

'Any word from Raven?'

'She's underground near the south exit,' Tech told him. 'Beowulf went to tell Leo, so she'll be here soon.'

'She's in safe hands with Leo.' Spartacus slid a sidelong glance at Kai. 'We hope!'

Kai began to fret as he imagined Leo close to Raven in the darkened tunnels.

Spartacus turned to Tech. 'There's something I have to do immediately after the fight but I'll be along to go over your edit as soon as I can.'

Tech smiled as Spartacus took his place at the bell beside the Cage. 'He thinks he's a hot-shot film editor as well as an army boxing champion.'

'I didn't know he was a boxing champion!' said Kai.

'He won some cup or other before his leg got damaged. Might have gone on to be really famous but that stopped everything. Boxing was his life. Said that losing his chance of being a professional fighter destroyed his whole future. He's very bitter about it.'

'How do you know this? He never talks to anyone.'

'I researched him before I agreed to work with him, and sometimes he lets things slip when he's pretending to edit my film.'

'*Pretending* to edit?' said Kai.

'Yeah. He's a control freak, so even though I've done all that's needed, he has to adjust or delete a few frames to show he's boss.' Tech shrugged. 'He's invested his money and is really on-side with the project. So I don't care as long as the overall content is up to my standards and the information about kids on the streets is included.'

'Are you a professional film maker?'

'I'd like to be. Want to do documentaries on social issues. Something that happened to my family while I was a paramedic made me volunteer to work in homeless shelters. Saw that younger and younger people were living below the poverty line. Began to take photos and make recordings. Thought I could give them a voice. I was filming Boudicca and Beowulf in a small gym that had been set up for troubled youth when Spartacus appeared. The organizers had asked him to help with the training and we got chatting.'

'But this isn't legal,' said Kai. 'Won't it mess up your chances for the future?'

'More likely the opposite,' said Tech. 'The publicity could be enormous.' He switched on the camera as the bell sounded for the first round.

Boudicca leaped forward, teeth bared.

'Oh!' Tech drew in his breath. 'What's she up to?'

The girls fought. Medusa, hissing, circled Boudicca, stretching and contorting her arms like writhing snakes. Boudicca pointed to her crown to show that she was Queen of the Cage, then she sliced and chopped aggressively, landing flat and edged blows. Spartacus encouraged posturing and theatricals. His strategy, which seemed to have paid off, was that the more dramatic the fight the more hits they'd get – and thus the money would increase.

Their rounds lasted only three minutes. Even in that short space of time, at the end of the first round Medusa was labouring. Boudicca's weight was telling heavily on the younger girl. Medusa barely lasted the second round – lagging well behind on points. Half a minute into the third and Boudicca had her in an armlock that she could not get out of.

Not even close.

Medusa submitted as the bell went. It was Boudicca's win. She would go through to fight against Raven in the girls' final the following evening.

Medusa's face was streaked green and grey, the painted snakes on her arms and legs blotched and distorted. She hesitated as if about to say something before she left the Cage. But with a grand flourish Spartacus announced the winner. Medusa climbed out as Boudicca pranced from corner to corner of the Cage, pirouetting so that Tech could get good shots of her front and back.

Tech was peering at his mini-screen. He looked un-happy.

'That was . . . different,' he said.

'What's different?' Kai asked.

'The way Boudicca was fighting. It might not be so apparent when you're standing far back, but with close-ups I can see it on the screen. At one point I thought she was going to bite Medusa.'

'You can't do that wearing a gum shield.'

'She didn't have one in,' said Tech. 'I noticed that at the start.'

'It must have fallen out by mistake.'

'Didn't look like a mistake, the way she came at Medusa in the opening seconds.'

Kai recalled the conversation in Tech's den after his fight with Leo earlier in the day when the Cage Fighters had discussed bending the rules. Boudicca had mentioned trying 'new moves' on Medusa. Had she decided not to wait for the nightly Meet? 'But' – Kai spoke slowly – 'before a fight Spartacus always checks our feet, hands, helmets – and mouths.'

Tech raised his eyebrows but didn't reply.

'In any case Medusa wasn't strong enough to resist Boudicca. So there was no call for Boudicca to get too physical.'

'But what if Medusa *had* been stronger?' Tech was still turning what he'd filmed over in his mind. 'Boudicca was . . . *is* . . . out to do damage.'

CHAPTER SIXTEEN

Kai was watching Tech finish off the edit of the girls' match when Raven and Leo arrived back.

'There he is,' Leo announced loudly, 'the Housing Officer for the London Underground!'

Kai was hoping that if he didn't respond Leo might shut up and leave him alone. But that didn't always work with Leo. He tended to pile on the snide remarks until he got a reaction.

'I hear you've collected another lame duck,' Leo persisted. 'You do appreciate that every extra person is a drain on resources? Why did you bring her into the tunnels?'

'You've no idea what's going on—' Kai replied angrily.

'Leo,' Raven cut across them, 'if me and Kai hadn't sorted out something for Bird Girl, then the rest of the fights would probably have been cancelled – tonight, tomorrow, and your finale with Kai on Saturday.'

'Of course!' Leo hardly missed a beat as he quickly changed tack. He appealed to Beowulf, who was still on monitor duty. 'Just joshing about,' he said. 'Banter, that's what.'

'Who is she anyway?' Beowulf asked. 'Are the rumours true? Did she really manage to take a photograph of one of us?'

'You can ask these questions in about ten minutes,' Spartacus said as he came into Tech's den carrying Bird Girl's rucksack. 'We'll have our Meet as soon as I've approved Tech's edit of the girls' match.'

Tech exchanged a look with Raven over Spartacus's head as he studied the film, making suggestions for alterations. By the time he was done the rest had arrived. Medusa was dejected by her defeat but Boudicca was on a high, talking louder than ever. Bird Girl, in the calming company of Sarema and Gita, seemed more settled. She gave Kai a weak smile when he brought her a stool.

Spartacus beckoned for her to sit beside him as he began the meeting. 'As you can see we have a guest, whose name is to be "Bird Girl". I'll bring you up to date on that situation after we do our business.' He went over the usual arrangements, allocating duties and updating information, including the timings for the last three matches. 'Tomorrow at midday Magog and Beowulf fight for third-place bonus; in the evening Raven and Boudicca fight to decide the girls' winner. Then' – he grinned at Leo and Kai – 'High Noon on Saturday is the final fight of the contest for overall boys' champion. Keep up your training,' he said. 'Give it all you've got.'

Kai saw Leo nod in response. On the surface it appeared he was talking to both boys but Kai was sure the last remark was a special word of encouragement for him.

'Anybody want to raise anything?' asked Spartacus.

'We're thinking of slackening our Fight Rules for the last matches,' said Boudicca. 'To make them more lively.'

'Interesting idea!' Spartacus exclaimed.

'Not everybody thinks so,' said Tech. 'For a Mixed Martial Arts fight to work you need rules and respect. Otherwise it's just a brawl.'

A tic crossed Spartacus's face. 'You're filming, not fighting, Tech, so you don't have a say – although I would have thought you'd see dramatic possibilities for the camera to capture.' As Tech started to reply Spartacus held up his hand. 'Only those in the Cage get to vote on this.' His eyes locked with Boudicca's.

'I'm for it,' said Boudicca. 'Definitely.'

'Me too.' As usual, Beowulf agreed with her.

'Well, I'm not,' said Medusa, glancing at Boudicca.

'Ah . . . Medusa . . . sorry. You can't vote on this either,' said Spartacus. 'You're out of the competition so you won't be in the Cage again.' He nodded confidently at Leo. 'Who else is for it?'

'I'm not scared of doing drama,' said Leo.

'That's my lad!' exclaimed Spartacus. 'Those *against*

pumping up the action for the last fights raise your hands.'

As Leo glowed under the praise a hollow thought entered Kai's heart – with no restrictions on Leo it would be like facing Evil Eddy in the Cage.

Magog put up his hand. 'I think we're doing fine the way we are.'

'I'm with Magog,' said Kai.

'Wimp!' Leo put his hand over his mouth to cover his remark.

Kai half rose to his feet.

Leo began to cough loudly as if he couldn't help it.

Tech's eyes were on Raven. He gave a shake of his head and visibly relaxed when she too raised her hand.

'It's a tie,' declared Spartacus. 'Three for the idea . . . and three against. Looks like I have to make a decision. Tell you what. I'll have a conversation with both fighters before each of the last three matches and we'll come to an agreement then. Bear in mind that we'd get more viewers if we upped the ante for the last fights.'

'We're getting stacks of viewers already,' said Raven. 'Before I came back in this evening I managed to catch the fight at a student hostel. It was amazing. Their TV lounge was standing-room only before the transmission time. While they were waiting for today's bout they ran some footage of the previous fights. Medusa – your snakes are spectacular.' She stretched out and fist-bumped Medusa. 'But this morning's re-run was the favourite. When I left they were still running it over and over in slow motion to see the moves. Leo, Kai' – Raven smiled at both of them – 'they love you guys. You should've heard the noise when Leo climbed up the cage. They were baying for blood!'

'Kai's or mine?' asked Leo. 'Mmmm . . . Let me guess. Whose profile pic gets most "likes"? Oh, that's right. It's mine!'

'And who does more talking than actual fighting?' Kai glared at him. 'Oh, that's right. It's you!'

'Doesn't matter,' Spartacus interjected. 'Anything that ups the interest will make the pay-per-views rise, and with it our income.'

'Tech, your edit is incredible,' Raven continued. 'You've cut the film at exactly the right spots. Scrolling the list of Fast Facts about kids living on city streets, and then revealing that it wasn't about a Third-World country, but right here in London, shocked the socks off them. And the music you added. Totally atmospheric. They were texting in donations like crazy.'

'I hope you've got some good shots of me winning *my* fight,' said Boudicca.

In answer Tech clicked the mouse and the wall screen filled with colour and movement – sinuous snakes and the golden twirling crown. There were great images of both girls, but, Kai noted, nothing to show the absence of Boudicca's gum shield. Tech must have deleted the one of Boudicca with her teeth bared before Spartacus had a chance to see it. The edited fight was fast and sharp, with lingering moments of Boudicca in her winning pose.

'You look awesome!' Beowulf told her.

Boudicca, who was watching for Leo's reaction, didn't hear him.

'Keep up the good work, Tech,' said Spartacus. 'But now there's another matter to deal with.'

Kai saw Bird Girl's face tighten.

'We have a . . . visitor. As I said previously, "Bird Girl" is what she is called, and while I'm relating her story I'm going to have Tech check out her laptop.' He pulled Bird Girl's rucksack from under his stool, opened it and gave the laptop to Tech.

When Spartacus had finished running through the info about Bird Girl, he turned to Tech again.

'So, what recent activity has taken place?'

'None.' Tech raised his head and addressed Spartacus. 'What do you mean "none"?'

Tech spread his hands over the laptop. 'Nothing has been sent out today. No emails. No social media contact whatever. No files downloaded. No files uploaded.'

'No files uploaded,' Spartacus repeated. He swung round on Kai. 'You told me that she'd sent her photos to her Cloud?'

'That's what she said she'd done!' Kai protested.

'And you took her at her word?' Spartacus spoke with heavy sarcasm.

'Better safe than sorry,' said Kai defensively.

'If you'd only checked then you'd have realized that all that was needed to contain the situation was to take her equipment. Bringing her here has given us complications.'

'We didn't have time to check! There was someone anxious to use the toilet!'

'Even if Kai had stolen my laptop and run off you would have had complications anyway.' Bird Girl's voice was thin but determined. 'I wouldn't have let this slide. I'd have reported it to the police and they'd have investigated further.'

Spartacus shook his head. 'No they wouldn't. They'd write it up as an ordinary street mugging. You were set upon by two junkies who saw your camera as an easy street flog for their daily fix. Happens a dozen times a day in the city. And you rabbiting on about what you saw . . . well, with no actual proof they're not going to deploy many officers for that. You said yourself they'd already had the wall examined. They'd probably have thought you were making the whole thing up to get attention.'

'I'd have gone to the newspapers,' Bird Girl insisted.

'Once they knew that transport workers had looked at the wall I doubt they'd have investigated further. If they decided it was worth a column or two, then, by the time they'd written it up, our cage fights would have been over, so no danger to us.' He turned to Kai. 'As I said, you should have taken her equipment and left her in the toilet. That would have been the best thing to do.'

'Maybe not.' Raven spoke up. 'She's completely obsessed about her sister. We offered to let her go in exchange for saying nothing but she refused. Even though I—'

'If we'd let her go,' Kai cut in before Raven could mention her knife in front of the rest of the group, 'she'd have bought herself a sledgehammer and smashed that brick wall apart.'

'And then there's this.' Raven took Bird Girl's phone from her pocket. 'She'd have called 999 and we might have been picked up by the police.'

Spartacus gave a curt nod. 'Still annoying though, with only two days to the end of the project. Let's see what she managed to record.' He took Bird Girl's phone and pressed 'play'.

A whispering voice began to speak:

'Please contact the police if you find this phone. I'm Maxine Carmey of 26, Mandor Close, London, looking for my sister Darcey. Am being held in an old skip near the—'

At this point Bird Girl had shoved her phone inside her shirt. Kai heard the muffled sound of him sliding down the chute into the skip and then silence. In the seconds after she'd gone over the top of the skip and before he followed her in, Bird Girl had set her phone to record.

'Is it true,' Leo asked in an overly innocent tone,

'that Raven had gone for help and Brainbox Boy was guarding the prisoner at the point when she was using her phone?'

Kai sucked in his breath and dug his nails into his palms to prevent himself from responding.

Spartacus affected not to hear the exchange, ran the audio track again and then pressed 'Delete'.

'So, *why* is this person here?' Boudicca raised her voice. She rounded on Kai and Raven. 'Why on earth did you guys decide to bring her in?'

Raven glowered at Boudicca. They were opposites in temperament – Raven quiet and secretive, Boudicca loud and brash.

'It was the safest thing to do,' said Raven.

'I'm not getting that.' Boudicca wouldn't back off. 'Neither am I getting why she agreed to come.' She addressed Raven. 'Did you threaten her?'

'I'll threaten you in a minute if you don't shut up,' Raven muttered.

Spartacus hadn't mentioned the part about the knife but Raven was known to defend her privacy aggressively. And it was obvious that something unusual had taken place.

'I wanted to come.' It was Bird Girl who stopped the argument escalating. 'I pleaded with Raven and Kai to take me with them. My sister thought a bird was caught behind the wall and I believe she found a way through there because she wanted to rescue it. And now I'm sure she herself is trapped and can't get out. I'm begging *all* of you for help.'

'But where's your proof?' Magog spoke in a reasonable manner. 'If there isn't anything on your laptop then you've only got your gut feeling.'

'We still haven't looked at my camera,' Bird Girl replied. 'As soon as I saw what I thought was a face I fired off a few shots before I ran to cross the road.'

'Ah . . .' said Spartacus, 'your camera . . .' He appeared downcast. 'The SD card must have got lost in the scuffle and so there's nothing to see, I'm afraid. Absolutely nothing.'

CHAPTER
SEVENTEEN

'Nothing?' The word was a strangled sound in Bird Girl's throat.

'Nothing,' Spartacus repeated firmly.

The colour left Bird Girl's face as if a grey cloth had wiped out her whole complexion.

Spartacus glanced at Leo.

'I'm OK with Bird Girl being here until Saturday evening,' said Leo, 'and then she can go out when we do. But it's almost lights-out time so I vote we end the Meet now.'

'My camera has a backup facility.' Bird Girl's voice was shaking. 'There can't be *nothing* on it.'

Spartacus shrugged. 'Must have been a malfunction. Not much anyone can do when that happens.'

'But . . . but I took photographs. Dozens of photographs.'

Spartacus shook his head.

Bird Girl turned to Tech. 'Surely there's a way of retrieving the images. You seem to be really skilled with things like this. If you could have a look at it—?'

'No!' Spartacus spoke before Tech could reply. 'There's no point in Tech doing that.' He made a small movement with his feet and Kai saw that he had tucked Bird Girl's rucksack further under his chair.

There was an awkward silence before anyone spoke.

'Shame,' said Magog. 'Sorry that happened.'

A couple chimed in with him. But generally there was a sense of relief that there was no extra problem to deal with before the closing fights.

'Yes indeed,' said Spartacus. 'We're *all* sorry for you, Bird Girl.'

'Well, that's that then,' Leo declared. 'We can't do anything more at the moment.'

Spartacus responded with an almost imperceptible nod. Kai switched his glance from one to the other. There was a self-satisfied smirk on Leo's lips. What had gone down there? Had Leo and Spartacus had a conversation before the meeting?

'You can remain here until the day after tomorrow,' Spartacus said to Bird Girl. 'Then you'll go topside with the rest of us and we wish you well in the search for your sister.'

There were murmurs of agreement, although Kai noticed that Raven hadn't joined in.

'But I took dozens of pictures,' Bird Girl repeated feebly. 'I don't understand . . .'

Kai stirred in his chair. His instinct was to go to her but something told him that would be the wrong thing to do.

'I want to leave now.' Bird Girl's voice was hardly above a whisper.

'I'm afraid that's not possible,' Spartacus said firmly. He looked around the room.

'No way,' said Boudicca. 'You might betray us. I didn't stay in this stink-hole for weeks so that you could waltz in here and wreck it all at the last minute. And anyway, you said that you wanted to come here.'

'You agreed to help me,' Bird Girl said to Spartacus.

'I said we would help you as far as we could,' he replied smoothly.

'You lied!'

'No, *you* lied,' he retorted. 'You told Raven and Kai that you'd uploaded a file to the Cloud and you hadn't. That lie is what caused them to bring you here. How many other lies are you telling?'

'How can we trust anything you say?' Leo asked Bird Girl. 'There's no proof that your sister is missing. No proof that you even have a sister. You could be an undercover cop.'

'I'm not a police spy,' said Bird Girl. She too looked around the room. Her eyes met Kai's but her gaze moved on to Raven. 'I do have a sister who has gone missing. Please believe me.'

'Well, if not a police spy,' said Boudicca, 'maybe you're from a different official organization.'

'Or a newspaper reporter?' suggested Leo.

'I am not a newspaper reporter,' Bird Girl responded.

'Well, whatever you are, the Cage Fighters get to decide what to do,' said Spartacus. 'It's up to them what happens to you. That's how it works here.'

Kai looked at the others. There was something off-key but he couldn't think what, exactly.

Medusa glanced at Raven and gestured a query with her hands. Raven frowned as if she was thinking hard.

'We need to keep her here,' said Boudicca.

'Yeah,' said Beowulf, agreeing with Boudicca like he always did.

'But safely,' said Magog. 'Nobody is to get hurt.'

'Of course not,' said Leo. 'But what can we do with her?'

'I don't know . . .' Spartacus hesitated. 'I suppose the only secure place is the storeroom.' He said this as if he'd only just thought of it.

'Are we saying she has to be kept locked up?' Magog asked. 'That's bit brutal.'

'It would only be for forty-eight hours,' Leo said quickly.

'There's plenty of food and drinks in there,' Boudicca backed him up.

'And magazines, and spare chemical toilet buckets,' added Medusa, trying to be kind.

'Let's have a show of hands then,' said Spartacus. 'Who thinks it safest to lock Bird Girl in the storeroom for the next forty-eight hours?'

Sarema moaned, 'No,' and Gita drew her shawl round her shoulders and shrank into herself. They were against anyone being kept against their will, but the twins didn't have voting rights.

'Wait a minute!' Bird Girl was struggling to compose herself. 'Before you vote, could Tech *please* take a look at my camera?'

'I don't mind doing that,' said Tech.

'There is nothing on the camera,' said Spartacus.

'But there should be, and Tech could search for the file, and—'

'I've done that,' said Spartacus tetchily. 'And we're wasting precious time on this. Believe me when I say that I know for definite that there are no photos in your camera.'

Bird Girl looked at Spartacus in horror. 'You deleted my photographs!'

'I may have made a mistake when trying to recover the file,' Spartacus said apologetically. 'I'm not good with technical equipment.'

'My precious photographs . . .' Bird Girl clutched her stomach as if in pain. 'You made me a promise that you'd try to help me and then you deleted the file.' She turned in anguish to Kai. 'You saw what I saw, didn't you?'

Kai hesitated. He was still trying to process what was happening in the room.

'Kai?' Bird Girl prompted him. 'You saw a face? Please tell them you saw a face.'

'Yes, Kai, tell us. Did you see a ghost?' Leo's voice was taunting. 'Is that what gave you such a fright and made you panic?'

'I *thought* I saw a face,' said Kai. He blew his breath out slowly from his mouth. 'But truthfully, now I'm not so sure.' He made a helpless gesture at Bird Girl. 'Maybe it was a nesting pigeon?'

'More likely a white plastic carrier bag,' said Leo. 'For whatever reason, Bird Girl's been faking this whole scenario.'

There was a horrible silence in the room.

And then Raven, who'd remained quiet throughout the whole debate, opened her mouth and spoke. In a carefully controlled voice she said, 'I picked this up from the toilet floor before we left the Internet café.' And reaching her fingers into the plait of her hair, she brought out a camera SD card.

Spartacus held out his hand. Raven looked to Tech who deftly took the SD card from Raven. Their fingers brushed together and a fleeting smile curved Raven's lips.

'Before you do anything with that—' Spartacus began. But he was too late. Tech had inserted the card into one of his machines, opened up the file and was clicking each icon.

There were a dozen or so pictures of pigeons. A few of the park, including the vagrant on the bench.

Only three images left.

From a distance, the bricked-up wall of the old Langsdaine Underground Station.

The second last photo zoomed in on a white mark in the wall.

'There!' breathed Bird Girl.

'It's a blob of nothing,' said Leo.

Then the last photograph was on the screen.

A full close-up of the space between two bricks.

And everyone could see what it was.

The blaze of white in the wall wasn't a bird or a white plastic carrier bag.

It was a human face.

CHAPTER EIGHTEEN

A wave of relief washed over Kai. Bird Girl wasn't lying! And, although he knew that the sight of this face on the screen brought a bunch of difficulties, he couldn't suppress a sense of happiness. Bird Girl had been telling the truth and it looked as if she had found her sister.

Bird Girl let out a long quivering breath. She stretched out her hand, fingertips reaching towards the blurred white outline of the face. And then she began to cry. A disturbing wild yowling, the like of which Kai had never heard before.

Sarema detached one of her scarves and handed it to Bird Girl, who buried her face in its folds as her sobs quietened down.

'She's not faking that,' said Kai.

The Cage Fighters hung about, not knowing what to do. Certain types of emotion weren't done in their group. People joked and laughed and squabbled and bickered – with Spartacus quick to quash anything that looked like it might develop into a real argument. But most of them didn't show their deeper feelings. Life on the street did that to you. Open emotions suggested weakness. Weakness attracted predators. Survival depended on building a hard shell around your heart and letting no one in.

Occasionally there'd be an echo in the tunnels at night and you'd know someone was having nightmares. But sadder, intimate thoughts were submerged. Spartacus emphasized there should be no whining, no sharing of woes. His advice was to recall the bad experiences of the past only as motivation to work towards a better future.

Now the Cage Fighters looked to Spartacus. Kai was aware that he was doing it too at this very moment – mentally and physically. The thought ran through his mind: we're so dependent on Spartacus. *Too much.* We depend on him for food, for water – without Spartacus we couldn't exist in the tunnels.

But it'd crept up to become more than the basics. The Cage Fighters depended on Spartacus for the purpose in their life, and with that went a whole raft of extra stuff. Spartacus didn't just direct what they physically did every day. Recently it was as if he was directing their thoughts too. And, with small unimportant variations, everyone went along with what Spartacus said.

Except.

The arrival of Bird Girl put that in jeopardy. Raven

giving the SD card to Tech was more than Raven's usual defiance. Kai began to understand the danger Bird Girl represented – why Spartacus wanted her contained until it was over. If he lost control of the Cage Fighters then the bonanza of the final money pay-off might never happen.

'That face is very indistinct. Do you recognize it as your sister?' Spartacus asked Bird Girl.

Bird Girl shook her head. 'But who else could it be?'

Spartacus stood up to hush the babble in the room. 'Does anyone know anything about this?'

'Not me!' Boudicca was the first to answer.

'Me neither,' said Magog.

Beowulf shook his head, as did Medusa.

'We all know it'd be foolish to go up that way,' said Leo.

'If anyone has done so, you *must* tell me.'

Spartacus made each one answer individually, including Tech. When he got to the twins Sarema said: 'It was only Kai, Raven and yourself who departed from the station via the monitored tunnels this day.' She pointed to Gita. 'My sister and I watch the small screens in Tech's den very diligently. Nobody else went along any of the tunnels until Raven returned to report to Spartacus.'

'The twins are good on the monitors,' said Tech. 'They notice everything. Report every movement to me, including when rats are on the move. Saw a badger once too.'

'OK.' Spartacus grunted at Tech. He was irritated

with him and Raven for their handling of the SD card but was attempting to keep a lid on it. 'Could that picture be some kind of animal?'

'No way.' Tech had enhanced the last image from the SD card and it sat on the big wall screen. Without doubt it was a human face.

'Could it be Mole?' asked Leo. 'He sneaks about without anyone seeing or hearing him.'

'Mole only comes up from the deeper tunnels when he needs supplies,' said Spartacus.

'And he knows every inch of the place so he'd never let himself be caught anywhere,' said Kai.

'What's on the log for that tunnel?' Spartacus asked Tech. 'When was it last used?'

'A week ago.'

'Is there a webcam there?'

'I've got one placed on the outside of Langsdaine Station – the same as I have on all disused stations in our area. It's a precaution so we'll get warning of possible intrusions like maintenance workers or Urban Explorers. That's how we picked up on someone' – he indicated Bird Girl – 'hanging about outside there.'

'And inside?' asked Spartacus. 'In the tunnel leading to the bricked-up wall?'

'There's no webcam,' said Tech. 'We lost the one that was there and didn't replace it. We haven't used that tunnel since—' He stopped and raised his eyebrows at Spartacus.

'Why not?' asked Bird Girl.

'It's too dangerous.' The words were out before Kai had calculated the effect they would have on her.

'Dangerous?' Bird Girl looked around the Group. 'Why? What makes it dangerous?'

No one answered her.

Bird Girl grabbed at Spartacus's arm. 'Why is it dangerous? Why did you stop using that tunnel?'

'The roof caved in a day or so ago,' said Boudicca. 'Well,' she said defiantly as a few people tutted at her, 'Bird Girl had to find out sooner or later. Better she knows what the situation is.'

'There's been a rockfall!' Bird Girl sprang to her feet. 'And my little sister is in there! She's probably trying to claw her way out right now while we sit around chatting.' Her voice rose higher. 'I don't care what you guys are involved in, but basically you seem like decent people. You can't leave her trapped in there to *die*.'

'Let's calm down while we think how to approach this situation.' There was a warning note in Spartacus's voice. He made a small signal and Boudicca and Leo got up and stationed themselves on either side of Bird Girl.

Kai's pulse began to accelerate. He glanced at Raven. Her face registered alarm. Was she in tune with his thoughts – that perhaps Spartacus had pre-arranged that Bird Girl would be detained and had organized Leo and Boudicca to help him?

Bird Girl didn't seem to notice the fact that she had

two guards beside her. She was tilting into hysterics. 'I'm going for the – the police right now! And, and, and, the fire brigade and, and . . .' She fell back onto her chair as she ran out of energy.

'There's one person who could sort this situation better than the emergency services,' said Tech.

'Who is that?' Bird Girl looked at Kai. 'Is it you?'

Kai shook his head.

'Who then?' asked Bird Girl.

'Mole,' Tech said softly.

'That weirdo,' said Leo. 'Mole the Mad? He's been underground so long he's beginning to look like his pet rat. Hair so blond it's almost white and those pink eyes. Gives me the creeps, so he does.'

'Mole is one of the most valued members of our group,' said Spartacus, glancing over his shoulder.

Kai knew why Spartacus was nervous. Mole had the habit of appearing and disappearing soundlessly without warning.

'Where is his den?' Bird Girl asked. 'I want to talk to him.'

'No one ever knows where Mole is,' said Kai. He had become quite friendly with Mole and knew that he never rested in the same place twice.

'That's right,' said Spartacus. 'Not even me. He lives separate from us. I'm not sure where.'

'Probably in some rats' nest,' said Leo.

Spartacus gave Leo a hard look. 'Without Mole we

wouldn't have found these tunnels or be able to survive in them. But I do have a way of contacting Mole – and after I refereed the girls' fight I went into one of the deeper tunnels he uses and left him a note asking him to come and see me whenever he could. I also asked him to investigate Langsdaine Station and explained why.'

'Oh.' Bird Girl sounded mollified. 'So you *were* trying to help me.'

Spartacus grimaced. 'I am not an unfeeling monster,' he said. 'But there was no point in raising hopes, when they might be dashed.'

'Why did you not tell us that at least?' asked Kai. 'That you'd sent for Mole?'

'Because I was trying to prevent a mood of hysteria.' Spartacus glanced at Raven with a disappointed expression. 'You should have handed over the SD card to me when we met up at the skip.'

'Forgot I had it.' Raven met his gaze and it was difficult to tell if she was lying.

'Hmm . . .' said Spartacus. 'In any case I believe we're all agreed that the best person to reconnoitre Langsdaine is Mole.'

'How can you be sure this person, Mole, will get the note?' asked Bird Girl.

'Mole's hearing is uncanny,' said Spartacus. 'He'll know I've been down in his sections and he'll go and find the message in our dead-letter box.'

'When will we see him?'

'Generally Mole turns up when we need him,' said Kai.

'Will he go to Langsdaine Station first, before he comes here?'

'You know what?' Boudicca broke in. 'She asks too many questions. She's only been here five minutes, and already she knows more about our set-up than some of us who've been here since the beginning. I think this whole thing is one big act. It's all too neat.' She shoved her face at Bird Girl. 'You faked that photo. You've come here to find out what we're doing and all this about a little sister is a load of guff.'

'I swear it's true.' Bird Girl looked frightened.

Boudicca loomed over her. 'She's lying about seeing a kid in that tunnel.'

'No, she ain't,' said a voice from the door. 'Whatever else she may be lyin' 'bout, she ain't lyin' 'bout that.'

CHAPTER NINETEEN

'Mole!'

Spartacus made his way across the room to where a skinny lad stood in the shadows of the door frame.

'I hate how he does that,' said Leo. 'It freaks me out the way he pops up without warning and it's obvious he's been secretly listening and spying on us.'

'People in glass houses . . .' murmured Kai, thinking of how Leo had wormed his way unseen into Tech's den after that morning's fight.

'What did you say?' Leo demanded.

'I'm saying people who find a new passageway' – Kai opened his eyes wide and copied Leo's earlier fake innocent tone of voice – 'are supposed to share that information. Not just appear in Tech's den by some mystery manner.'

Leo's reaction surprised Kai. Instead of being embarrassed he laughed in delight. 'You've not checked the Main Map as often as you should, Brainbox Boy! 'Cos if you did, you'd see a new line there. It doesn't lead outside, so not much use to claustrophobics like yourself.'

'Rein it in, you guys,' said Beowulf. 'We've got other stuff to sort out now.'

'Hi there, Mole.' Spartacus was speaking in a friendly manner. His voice was always pleasant, almost deferential, when he was with Mole. He never gave him orders like he did the others. 'Can you help us out here? Do you know anything about what's going on up at the closed-off Langsdaine Station entrance?'

Mole raised his scrawny arm and pointed at Bird Girl. 'What she says be true. There be a someone on the inside of the wall at Langsdaine.'

'Is it my sister? Have you seen her? Have you spoken to her? Is she OK?' A stream of questions fell in a gibberish flow from Bird Girl's mouth.

'Quiet!' Spartacus said in a low but firm voice. He addressed the Cage Fighters who were chattering amongst themselves. 'All of you. *Please* be quiet.' As they fell silent he went on, 'I will ask the questions. Don't anyone, *anyone*,' he repeated, staring at Bird Girl, 'speak or move until I say they can. Otherwise I will take Mole to my den and interview him myself.'

While Spartacus was speaking Mole reached into his breast pocket and took out a large white rat which he placed on his shoulder. Mole stroked the rat as it nuzzled at his ear.

'Would you like to come into the room?' Spartacus asked Mole. 'Then we can hear more clearly what you have to say.'

Mole inclined his neck towards the rat as if listening to it. 'Albert says "no". Albert says there be folks here who don't like Albert.' He squinted his eyes at Leo.

Leo stared back at him.

'OK, OK,' Spartacus said. 'I appreciate bright light hurts your eyes so you remain where you're most comfortable.'

'Albert and I be doin' that,' said Mole.

Spartacus waited, and then, as Mole offered no more information, he asked, 'When did you discover that there was someone on the inside at Langsdaine?'

'Yesterday, but wuzn't sure.'

'And now you are sure?'

'Set out some bait so I did. Just back from checkin' on it. Choccy bikkies all gone.'

'Don't rats eat biscuits?'

'They do. But no rat I know does take the paper off choccy bikkies afore eatin' them.'

'Darcey adores chocolate biscuits,' Bird Girl whispered.

'That I do ken,' said Mole. He smiled at Bird Girl. 'For she bin eatin' six of them already.'

'So she's not starving then?' Bird Girl asked.

'She be not hungry,' said Mole. 'She bring good supplies for camp-out. She be makin' herself a neat ickle den up there.'

'Thank you for looking after my sister,' said Bird Girl. 'And . . . and Albert too.'

Mole moved from the shadows and pushed his shoulder forward. 'Would thee like to stroke Albert?'

'Yes, I would.' Bird Girl slowly approached Mole. Without hesitating she reached out a finger and rubbed the rat gently between his ears.

Kai saw Spartacus ball his hands into fists. Bird Girl had disobeyed his command to neither speak nor move until he said so. But Mole was content talking to her and Spartacus couldn't interfere without the risk of upsetting him.

'Your sister she do like birds,' said Mole.

'Yes, she does.' Silent tears coursed down Bird Girl's cheeks. 'Ever since she was small, she loved watching birds.'

'She be feedin' some nestlings. To keep them alive.'

'So Darcey was right! A nest had fallen down inside the wall and the chicks were trapped inside?'

Mole nodded.

'I must go and speak to her,' said Bird Girl.

'Not good.' Mole shook his head. 'Not good.'

Bird Girl bit her lip. 'Why not?'

'Albert tell me she will not leave there until the chicks do fly. Only Albert must come. If anyone else, she will run off and never come back. Not ever.'

'Jeez-oh!' muttered Leo. 'Now he thinks his rat can talk.'

'How do you know this?' asked Spartacus. 'How can you have given her biscuits? I myself went up and had a look at this side of the collapsed section. The rubble is so densely packed that there's no space for anyone to get in or out of there.'

'No space for a human.' Mole gave Spartacus a cunning look. 'Plenty space for a rat.'

'Albert?' Bird Girl looked more closely at the white rat. 'Oh!' she said. 'There's a tiny camera on Albert's collar!'

'Albert be the best tunneller. He show me the way through when I do dig.'

'He's very clever,' said Bird Girl.

'Albert do carry messages too.' And from his trouser pocket, Mole produced a crumpled sheet of paper.

CHAPTER TWENTY

Spartacus ground his teeth in frustration as Mole handed the note to Bird Girl.

'Read that out so that I know what it says,' he said.

Bird Girl avoided Spartacus's gaze.

'Please,' he added in the nicest voice he could muster. 'To keep us safe underground it is our policy to share all information.'

Raven sniffed loudly, but even she wasn't bold enough to mention the fact that Spartacus hadn't been sharing everything.

There was silence while Bird Girl read and re-read the note to herself.

'Our normal procedure has been disrupted,' Spartacus said in a placating tone. 'In these exceptional circumstances I decided it wouldn't be wise for me to let the Cage Fighters know that I had inspected the Langsdaine tunnel and couldn't see a way through the blockage. I didn't want anyone organizing a search party and running up there to tear at the stones. It might have brought the whole roof in. I viewed all aspects and came to the conclusion that, before we did anything, Mole should be consulted.'

'And you were right.'

To Kai's surprise it wasn't Leo or Boudicca who had spoken up for Spartacus. It was Bird Girl.

'By asking Mole for help Spartacus did work out the best plan to help my sister.' Bird Girl held up the note. 'You'll see what I mean when I read you what's written on this piece of paper.'

How you be?

'Was it you who wrote that?' Bird Girl asked Mole. When he nodded she went on. 'My sister has written her reply below Mole's question.'

I am very well. Thank you for sending the White Rat with biscuits for me. Please send bread for the baby birds as I did not bring enough and they won't eat chocolate. They are very hungry. I am staying here until they can fly. Then I will take them outside. Do not tell the police or my big sister where I am. If you do I will run away into the deep tunnels and not come out. Not ever.

When she'd finished, Bird Girl looked at Spartacus. 'You don't need to lock me up,' she said. 'I'm not leaving here until my sister agrees to come with me.' She wiped her face with Sarema's scarf to dry off her tears and sweat. 'I'll wash this before I return it to you,' she told Sarema.

Sarema glanced at Spartacus before replying. 'It is my gift to you. We rejoice that your sister is found.'

'How did she get to where she is?' Spartacus asked Mole.

Mole tapped his forehead with his finger. 'She be smart,' he said.

'But,' Spartacus addressed Bird Girl, 'I thought you said your sister had special needs?'

'She has, but she's clever in her own way,' said Bird Girl.

'We all be clever in our own way,' said Mole. He touched his rat on the nose. 'Albert be clever in his own way.'

'Darcey loves secret places,' Bird Girl explained. 'When she was small her favourite place to play was inside a cupboard or under the table. She could find her way out of a maze in minutes and would crawl among the bushes in the park for hours on end.'

Bushes in the park! Kai suddenly remembered the trainers near the manhole cover in the park bushes.

'Ah!' The same thought had occurred to Raven. She waved her hand at Spartacus. 'I've just realized that there was something different in the bushes when Kai and

I went out through the manhole cover in Langsdaine Park. A pair of trainers that had been lying about there were placed neatly together.'

'That's exactly what my sister would do!' Bird Girl exclaimed. 'She can be obsessively tidy.'

'Dove must have found the manhole in the bushes in Langsdaine Park and worked out how to get to the other side of the wall,' said Kai.

'And then the roof came down!' Bird Girl turned to Mole. 'Is there a risk of another cave-in? How can we rescue her?'

Mole hesitated for half a second. 'Make roof safe first. Then she can get out.' He pointed at the crumpled paper in Bird Girl's hand. 'I be writin' her and tyin' bread to Albert's collar.'

Reluctantly Bird Girl handed over the note, and Mole took a pencil stub from his pocket and spoke aloud as he wrote:

Albert bring bread

'Tell her I love her,' said Bird Girl. 'That it doesn't matter what's she's done. That I'm not angry with her. That—'

'Mole can't write that,' Kai interrupted in a quiet voice. 'Your sister said that if anyone told you where she was she'd go further underground. We know that she's capable of doing that. Best let Mole deal with this.'

Mole looked at Bird Girl. 'Kai be right. Not good for Mole to write what you say.'

Bird Girl hung her head. 'OK,' she said.

'I've an idea.' Tech held his hand up.

Spartacus hesitated and then said, 'Go ahead.'

'We could run a line in there with another tiny camera and audio link and ask her to set it up so that she can talk to Mole. Then Bird Girl would be able to see Dove without her sister knowing she's there. I could attach it to Albert's collar, if that's OK with you, Mole?'

Mole leaned his head towards his rat. 'Albert say "yes".'

'Do you think Dove would accept that?' Kai asked Bird Girl.

'We could tell her that it would help keep the birds alive,' suggested Raven.

Bird Girl shot her a look of gratitude. 'Mole, if you mentioned the birds then she might co-operate.'

Mole licked the end of his pencil and laboriously wrote out the message. Then he rolled it up and tucked it under Albert's collar.

'Need bread,' he said. 'And wood for roof props.'

'Help yourself to whatever from the storeroom,' said Spartacus. 'I'll lend you the key.'

'Beats me why *he* gets the key and free run of the storeroom when the rest of us don't,' said Leo.

'Don't need no key to get into the storeroom.' Mole tapped his finger on the side of his nose, before fading into the shadows by the door.

'I'll go and see if Mole needs a hand with anything and come back in a few minutes to collect the film file of the girls' fight,' said Spartacus hurriedly. 'One last thing before you leave,' he added as the Cage Fighters started stacking their stools. 'No one' – he fixed his gaze on Bird Girl – 'I repeat, *no one*, must go near that rockfall without my permission. If they do I will personally lock them up without further discussion.' His face softened. 'Please listen to me.' He looked directly at Kai and Raven. 'It's for your own safety; we're all in this together.'

CHAPTER TWENTY-ONE

There was a tangible lifting of tension in the room as Spartacus went out of the door.

Bird Girl loosened the scrunchie that held her hair. She gathered up the ends that had straggled free and swept the whole lot back off her face to redo her ponytail. Then she swiped Sarema's scarf across her face once more.

'I hope you are feeling better now, Bird Girl,' Sarema said politely.

'Yes, thanks . . . thanks very much.' While she was speaking Bird Girl's eyes roved the room and came to rest on Kai, Raven and Tech.

Raven slithered her stool towards Tech's worktop. 'Ace idea about running the line in. What are you going to use?'

Kai looked at her in slight surprise. Within the space of an hour Raven had made two positive remarks.

'Dunno, exactly,' said Tech. He grinned at Raven. 'Felt I had to say something before Spartacus exploded.'

'If anyone can get a sight and sound link in there, it's Mole,' said Kai.

Tech was rooting in his boxes and shelves, assembling wire, cable and pieces of electronic equipment. 'We need to set up lighting too so that we can keep watch on the area.'

'Mole will have to be coaxed to do that,' said Kai. 'He hardly ever uses torches when he's in the tunnels.'

'Yeah, he's well-named,' said Leo. 'Even looks like a mole with that snout of his twitching away.'

'Why is Mole in the tunnels if he's not a Cage Fighter?' asked Bird Girl.

'He be a-diggin' fur gold.' Leo mocked Mole's speech as he answered her.

'Really?' Bird Girl turned to Kai. 'Does Mole actually think that there's gold down here.'

'He don't be thinkin' it.' Leo laid his finger along the side of his nose. 'He be *knowin'* it.' And he laughed loudly as he left the den.

Kai nodded his head. 'Mole's been living in these tunnels for ages. Said his grampa sheltered here when he was just a boy – during the Blitz in the Second World War. His grampa told him that he and his brother went exploring one night when the adults were asleep. They crawled through an air vent and found a whole stash of gold: bars and sovereign coins. Reckoned it was connected to the secret bunker where Churchill and the War Cabinet held meetings to be safe from the bombs. They worked out that it was probably a hoard to help the Resistance if Britain was invaded. His grampa and his brother went to find it a few nights later, but there was another bombing raid on London and an unexploded bomb was lying in the way. Saw the tail fin sticking out of the debris. They were going back up the tunnel to report it when there was an explosion. They were lucky to survive. When they next managed to return, the whole area was blocked. Mole's grampa made a map 'cos he reckoned that the gold was still buried under there.'

'Why didn't Mole's grampa go tunnelling when the war was over?'

'There was a sudden heavy raid one night and Mole's grampa's family didn't get to the shelters. His grampa's parents and brother were killed and Grampa himself was taken in by relatives out in the country. When he came back into London as an adult, he tried to locate the place using the map he'd made as a child.'

'He'd made a sort of treasure map?'

'Exactly. Mole's grampa got a job working for London Underground so he could research every line, vent and crawlspace. Mole was brought up by his grampa. I don't think he was in school much – told me they spent most of their days in the tunnels. Said his grampa was obsessed with finding the hidden gold.' Kai shrugged. 'I guess he passed on his obsession to Mole.'

'So Mole has nothing to do with Spartacus or the *Cage Fighters for Freedom* project?'

Kai shook his head. 'I'm not quite sure how they met up, but in exchange for supplies Mole led Spartacus to this abandoned Tube station where we could make an HQ and build dens. He gave us a map of entry and exit routes. He never goes to the surface at all now 'cos Spartacus keeps him stocked up with food and water, and' – Kai recalled the boxes in the lock-up – 'digging tools. Every time you meet him he says he's almost reached the treasure.'

'Do you reckon it's true?' Raven asked Tech. 'That there's this stash of gold still buried underground?'

'Nah,' said Tech. 'Spartacus told me that there were tons of bunkers containing various items hidden under the London streets, but after the war they were removed so the Underground transport system could be extended. He reckons that the Ministry of War would have taken the gold right out of there when the bomb landed. Then they probably exploded the bomb deliberately to cover any trace of the secret location. And even if it didn't happen that way, there was always a record of these stores. He said that, with modern technology, it would have been recovered by now.'

The Cage Fighters started to disperse. Sarema and Gita, who did their monitoring duty together, took their places for the night shift. As Bird Girl moved her stool beside them she asked Kai a question:

'Do you think Mole will do what he said he would tonight? Make contact with my sister again?'

'Definitely,' said Kai. 'In the weeks we've been here I'm the only Cage Fighter who liked to go topside as much as I could. Often Mole would pop up and keep me company along the route. I've got to know him and he's a genuinely nice person. I'd trust him completely.'

'Thanks . . . for everything.' Bird Girl raised her hand as if she would touch Kai's face. Then she let it drop by her side.

Tech checked his watch. He patted Raven on the shoulder. 'You should get some rest 'cos you're fighting tomorrow.'

'Let's hope Bird Girl is happier now that Mole is on the case,' Kai said, falling into step beside Raven as she headed towards her den.

'Yeah,' said Raven. 'Bird Girl being happy – that's my biggest hope of the year!'

Kai twisted his head to look at her. 'What's up? Is my talking about Bird Girl annoying you?'

'Bird Girl, Bird Girl, Bird Girl. Every sentence you say recently has her name in it. How could that possibly annoy anyone?'

'She doesn't mean anything to me.' Kai's voice came out less convincing than he intended. It wasn't true that Bird Girl meant nothing to him. He had sympathy for her mission to find her sister and felt some responsibility for bringing her underground. Kai attempted to explain his thoughts. 'I suppose I do feel drawn to her, but that's not the same as the feelings I have for you. What we have is special.'

Ravens stopped and rounded on Kai. 'We don't have anything special. Don't ever think that we do, Kai. I don't do "special" feelings for anyone. I'm no one's "special" girl.'

'OK, OK.' Kai tried to lighten the tone. 'In that case, why is it when I mention her name it bothers you so much?'

'Her name!' said Raven. 'Exactly that! I am the girl who can fly. The one person here who chose to be a bird. A bird with wings. And I was the only bird girl until she arrived.'

'Oh,' said Kai, 'I see.' Now he understood Raven's irritation. It wasn't the sting of love rivalry that was riling her. It was jealousy over the name. 'I'm sorry. When I called her "Bird Girl", I wasn't thinking too deeply. It was because she was taking photographs of those birds in the park.' He tried to make a joke. 'Stupid pigeons. Waddling about. Can't fly without bumping into things. A pigeon isn't a proper bird. The cartoons of pigeons in Mary Poppins look more like real birds than actual pigeons do. No one takes pigeons seriously.'

They'd reached Raven's den. She unlocked it and went inside. Sitting on her bed she unpinned her hair grips. Raising her face to the ceiling she shook her head. Her hair cascaded out, a sleek and shining ebony waterfall down her back. It draped over her shoulders, covering the thin straps of her fight vest and merging with the detailed feathered wings painted on her back and arms. When she moved, her hair and skin rippled as feathers in a gentle breeze.

'Look in your mirror, Raven,' Kai said softly. 'There's only one Cage Fighter who is truly a bird, and her name is Raven.'

CHAPTER TWENTY-TWO

The next morning Kai went to relieve Medusa, who'd taken over from the twins during the early hours. Tech was still asleep in his curtained-off bunk so they chatted in whispers before she left.

'Everything was quiet in the tunnels last night,' Medusa told Kai, 'apart from Mole going backwards and forwards to Langsdaine with material from the storeroom. He took his last load up at five a.m. and he's still there.'

'He's probably working,' said Kai. 'I'm not sure he ever sleeps.'

'Well, you know him better than anyone.' Medusa hesitated. 'Kai . . .'

'What?'

'Watch out when you're in the Cage with Leo for the final fight.'

'I'm always on the alert with that sneaky beggar,' said Kai.

'I know,' said Medusa, 'but be especially so now.'

'Why especially now?'

'Things have changed – in the Cage, I mean. When I was fighting Boudicca I was almost glad I was weaker than her. I felt that if I'd been able to resist then she might have . . . I don't know . . . done something . . . cruel.'

'Don't worry. I'll be ready for Leo,' said Kai. 'But anyway, Spartacus said he'd go over the rules with us before we fight.'

'Yeah . . . right.'

'Everything OK?' Tech appeared, yawning, from his bunk.

Kai updated him. 'Mole seems to have spent the night at Langsdaine.'

'He must have decided it was more important to make the roof safe before running the cable in.' Tech pointed to the carrier bag he'd filled with surveillance equipment which was still on his worktop.

'And to let Dove sleep?' suggested Medusa.

'Hope Bird Girl managed to get some rest too,' said Kai.

'You're very concerned about her, aren't you?' Medusa gave Kai a mischievous look.

'Brought some breakfast for you guys!' Raven came in and plonked a tray of muffins and coffee on Tech's workshop. 'Don't do your usual guzzle of the chocolate-chip ones please, Tech.'

'Too busy trying to make a good profile for you when you're such a difficult subject,' Tech teased her back.

He was on his keyboard experimenting with sound and visuals. A ball of phosphorous light rotated on the big screen. To the clamour of beating wings and wildly cawing crows Raven stepped from the centre. Clad in black leather trousers and thigh-high boots with wings arching above her shoulders she strode towards the camera.

'Fabulous!' said Raven.

Their heads bent close as they became absorbed in weaving sound and visuals together.

Sitting at the monitor gave Kai time to think. Medusa had been warning him about Leo. As if he needed any warnings about being wary of unexpected violence. That had been the pattern of his life before he'd run away from home. And he realized that he'd begun to collude in it. To avoid involving his mum in any confrontation with Eddy he'd make up stories to explain new bruises by mentioning rough tackles at football practice or a fall from a skateboard.

Kai's mind was still in turmoil when Boudicca arrived ahead of schedule for her shift on the monitor. 'Oh!' Her face clouded with disappointment. 'I thought Leo was on duty.'

'No sign of Mole coming back yet.' Kai gave her the handover report.

'OK.' Boudicca glanced to the door. 'Wonder where Leo is . . .'

'He was in the café, deep in conversation with

Spartacus, when I was getting the breakfast muffins,' said Raven.

'Didn't ask you,' Boudicca retorted.

'Thanks for coming in early.' Kai stood up to give her his stool. 'It means I can watch the fight between Magog and Beowulf.'

'I'd better get along to the Arena.' Tech picked up the camcorder and slung the strap across his shoulder.

'Hang on until I fix this for you.' Raven reached up with both hands and straightened the strap around Tech's neck.

Kai imagined what it would be like to have Raven's arms around his own neck. Then he blinked the thought away and they were walking out of the den.

Spartacus was standing outside the Cage speaking to both boys. Beowulf was nodding but Magog was shaking his head. Leo joined them and it seemed that, whatever the discussion, Magog was the only one disagreeing.

'What's happening?' Tech asked Leo as he broke away and came over to them.

'Spartacus wants to inject some "pizzazz" – as he put it – into what could otherwise be rather a dull fight. Beowulf was up for it but Magog is refusing.'

'What kind of "pizzazz"?' asked Tech.

'Magog is never going to win this,' said Leo, 'so he'll be on the lowest bonus payment. You'd think he'd be happy to do anything to get more cash.'

'It's not always good to do anything for more cash,' Raven commented.

Tech focused the camera on Beowulf and his breath whistled from between his teeth. 'He's not wearing a gum shield either!'

'Get your camera ready,' joked Leo, 'in case he sinks his choppers into Magog's neck!'

Tech ignored him and walked with Kai to the far side of the Cage, where Spartacus was introducing the fighters.

'From the Land of Giants, we have Magog! Our Man Mountain and Grisly Gargantuan who guards London!'

The gold braid on Magog's green and crimson tunic glinted in the light as he stood in the centre of the Cage. Casting aside his staff and cloak, Magog beat his chest with his fists.

'And now, our Demon Destroyer! Bold Beowulf from the Badlands!'

Beowulf somersaulted into the Cage and stood up. He was dressed in criss-crossed laced leggings, with a multitude of intricate whorls and knots and magic symbols inked on his helmet, vest and body.

'Can the Colossus crush the brawny Beowulf?' Spartacus's voice resounded around the Arena. 'Or will Brave Beowulf bring down the Magnificent Magog?'

The bell rang, and the fight began. Magog was taller, but hadn't the speed of Beowulf, nor the experience to counter blows from an opponent who was left-handed.

Swinging his fists, he lumbered about the Cage while Beowulf evaded him. When it was his turn to fight Magog, Kai had gone easy on the big guy as he was aware that Magog was the rawest recruit to the project and had little training.

This fight was going in a different direction. In the first minute Beowulf had bested Magog, flooring him with a double leg takedown. But strangely, he didn't follow through. Instead he skipped away to his own corner, dallying until the end of the round.

In the second round, Beowulf put a choke hold on Magog. He released his grip almost at once, so that Magog, who by now had a bemused look on his face, was able to carry on until the bell sounded.

'What's going on?' Kai asked Tech. 'Do you think Spartacus asked them to spin it out?'

'If he did' – Tech's attention was on the screen of the camcorder – 'then I don't think Magog is in on it. Beowulf's baiting him, playing a game of cat-and-mouse.'

'Spartacus has to have awarded higher points to Beowulf in the first two rounds,' said Kai. 'Maybe Beowulf will let Magog get some strikes in the third so he's not completely put down.'

'Don't think so.' Tech shook his head. 'Beowulf's saving something for the finish.'

The bell rang.

Beowulf sprang from his stool and within seconds he was in under Magog's guard – their bodies so close that

Magog hadn't room to use his height and longer reach to his own advantage. Beowulf aimed a right-handed punch. Magog blocked by raising his own right arm.

Leaving his back exposed.

Beowulf pivoted and, with all his strength behind it, drove a thunderous left hook towards Magog's ribs.

'Jeez!' Kai exclaimed. 'A liver shot!'

Magog doubled up in excruciating pain. His legs folded beneath him and he crumpled to the floor.

Spartacus declared a Technical Knock Out and awarded the win to Beowulf.

'There was no need for that extreme viciousness!' Kai had never seen Tech so rattled as he snapped the camera closed. 'This isn't what I wanted to film and promote.'

It should mean nothing to Kai who won this contest, yet he was unhappy. The atmosphere was curdled. Was it the way Beowulf was swaggering about the Cage? But why shouldn't he? He'd won third place. It was his right to show off.

But . . . there was a definite change among the fighters. Spartacus would blame Bird Girl, even though she was less disruptive now that she trusted Mole to make sure her sister was OK. Maybe it was the prospect of the bonus money that was bringing out bad feeling?

CHAPTER
TWENTY-THREE

As they left the Arena Kai noticed that Leo had dropped his pace to be level with Raven.

'Just wanted to thank you again for the new bottle of special orange nail varnish,' he said.

Kai zoned out the noise around him so that he could hear their conversation.

'I assumed you wouldn't manage to get it,' Leo went on, 'with the nuisance of getting caught up in another of Kai's missions of mercy.'

'After I sent the last text from Bird Girl's phone I did a detour to the only shop I know that sells it,' said Raven. 'Bought you half a dozen bottles so you won't run out.'

'I've only one more big fight to go,' said Leo.

'Yeah. But after this is over you might want to keep on wearing it.' Raven smiled at him. 'Definitely your thing!'

'Wish I was better at applying nail varnish.' Leo splayed his fingers to show his nails. 'It goes on so blobby when I do it. *And* I make a mess over my fingers.'

'I'll paint your nails for you if you like,' Raven offered.

'Would you?' Leo threw Kai a mocking smile. 'I'd be ever so grateful.'

A jealous pang jumped through Kai. As Raven and Leo peeled off towards her den Kai kicked at a stone lying on the ground ahead of him. He decided to go to the café where Bird Girl and the twins were eating lunch.

He slumped into a chair. Even Gita sliding a snack bar across the table could hardly raise a smile. Kai waved a thanks for the bar at her, and then shoved it in his pocket.

Spartacus was discussing the audio track with Tech, but he paused as he walked past. 'I'm calling our Meet earlier today. We'll have it before Raven and Boudicca's fight tonight. I've left a note for Mole asking him to report back to us then.' He nodded at Bird Girl. 'I went into the Langsdaine tunnel this morning. He's getting that roof well propped up.'

'Thank you,' Bird Girl replied in a polite voice.

'Meanwhile, I've got to go out to post this fight so I'm relying on you, Kai, to keep an eye on things. I need to know that I can trust you.'

'You can trust me!' Kai said indignantly. 'Of course you can.'

Spartacus gave him a long look. 'We're side by side on

this journey, Kai,' he said. 'Please don't let me down again.'

There was silence at the table for a minute after Spartacus left and then Bird Girl said, 'I'm curious about the name of your leader.'

'Why?' Kai asked.

'You each choose your own name. Right?'

'Uh,' said Kai. His eyes were on Raven and Leo where they'd stopped outside her den. Leo was adopting his usual posture of leaning up against a wall. He was taller than Raven and he'd placed his arm and hand high above her head. Kai saw him manoeuvre his position so that Raven was under his arm. It looked as if he was protecting her.

More than that. As if they were an item.

Together.

'Has he ever said what made him decide to call himself "Spartacus"?'

'Wha-at?' Kai refocused himself.

'Spartacus,' Bird Girl repeated, 'your leader. Why did he choose "Spartacus" for his name?'

'Spartacus was some kind of super-dude slave,' said Kai. 'He lived in ancient times and fought as a gladiator. So the name is appropriate. Spartacus bonded the rest of the slaves together. They escaped and he led them in a revolt against their Roman masters.'

'But . . . you *do* know what happened to them in the end?' As Kai didn't answer Bird Girl went on, 'Ultimately

Spartacus failed. He was killed. His followers were captured. Most were executed.'

Kai laughed. 'Well, that's not going to happen to us. We've each got our plans made for when we leave the tunnels.'

'What are the arrangements for that?'

'We separate, and then meet Spartacus and Tech in a month's time to collect further payments from the pay-per-view hits. But on Saturday evening we get the money we've made so far. After that share-out the Cage Fighters take their designated routes out of here.'

'Just like that?' asked Bird Girl.

'Why not?'

'Think about it, Kai. Groups going to the surface together will be noticeable no matter what exits you use.'

Kai reflected for a minute. From the beginning Spartacus had discouraged anyone going above ground. If it was absolutely necessary to do so – when Magog's special mouth guard had needed replacing, for instance – then it was never more than two people at any one time. For safety's sake, Spartacus had said. As the days passed it was mainly Kai who went topside as he had issues with being confined. But Kai trusted Spartacus. And Spartacus had faith in Kai. What had he said to Kai before going to help Tech with the edit?

Kai, please don't let me down again . . .

As if she'd sensed his thoughts Bird Girl continued, 'Spartacus uses emotional manipulation to keep people in line. He's very good at appealing to your sense of decency and making you feel you owe him your unswerving loyalty.'

'We *do* owe him,' said Kai. 'Every one of the Cage Fighters owes him for helping them get off the streets.'

'You act as though he's giving you something for nothing and so you can't question him.'

'He's interested in helping young people who've nowhere to go. Spartacus is trying to draw attention to how many kids are living rough.'

Kai became aware that Sarema was listening attentively. Raven was rebellious, but Sarema was the only one who questioned Spartacus on a thoughtful level. She moved closer to them.

'All of that is Tech's idea.' Sarema hardly moved her lips as she spoke. 'His young sister was a troubled soul. She ran away and was found dead on a London street. Tech wants to help others like her. It's the reason he is underground doing this work. He sees you fighting in the Cage like a metaphor for how we have to live our lives. That's why he splices in information on homeless young people. It is Tech who has the strong social conscience, not Spartacus.'

'How do you know this?' Kai asked her.

'Gita and I spend many hours on the monitors. Sometimes when Spartacus is having discussions with Tech he forgets we are there.'

'After the final fight the Cage Fighters will be carrying money,' said Bird Girl. 'More money than you've had for years, or ever in your lives. A few of you might save it for the future but one or two won't be able to resist a spending spree. I know that the body paint worn by Raven, Beowulf and Medusa isn't permanent – but it makes them recognizable. It will attract attention and you guys could be rounded up in days.'

'So what? Cage fighting and being in the tunnels may not be strictly legal but it's not a grave offence. What would they charge us with?'

'Trespassing on railway property?'

'Spartacus said they tried that with an Urban Explorer and lost the case,' said Kai.

'This is different,' Bird Girl said stubbornly. 'You've set up an HQ here and are taking part in unlicensed boxing. You're using electricity without paying. By living underground you could be considered a security risk. If Spartacus really had your best interests in mind he'd not let you go up top when it's over and stroll about anywhere.'

'Spartacus was suspicious of *you*,' said Kai. 'But now you're more suspicious of *him*.'

Sarema half covered her mouth with her scarf as she poured the tea. 'Perhaps Bird Girl's words are wise.'

'What's going on here?' Kai said in exasperation. 'You guys are the ones with the most to be thankful for, and yet you're showing the least appreciation.'

'Outsiders watching what is happening may have a clearer view than those who are living within a situation,' said Sarema.

'And there's the money,' said Bird Girl.

'What about the money?'

'For Spartacus to have set this up and invested so much time and money he must have a plan where he makes more than anyone else.'

'He's been quite open about that,' said Kai. 'He gets the biggest percentage of the pay-per-views because he bought the supplies and equipment to set up the project. And the bank accounts are in Tech's name. Money can't be taken out without him signing a withdrawal slip.'

'I just think that, for Spartacus to go to all this bother, there has to be a wodge of extra cash coming to him from somewhere,' said Bird Girl. 'Also . . .' She paused. 'There's another thing that's been troubling me, something a lot more serious . . .' Her voice faded.

'What do you mean by "something a lot more serious"? Go on.' Kai was becoming irritated. 'Tell me. What's been troubling you?'

'If I'd not passed his "Tunnel Entrance Exam" in the lock-up, what would he have done with me? What if I hadn't agreed to come underground and behave myself? I knew too much for him to let me go. What would Spartacus have done with me?'

It was a question that Sarema had asked Kai. *What would have become of us if you had not forced Spartacus to take us in?* He'd thought Sarema meant if they'd been left in the skip, so he hadn't replied because he didn't want to say that Gita would most likely have died and

Sarema might have died too if she'd stayed with her sister. Now he realized that Sarema meant: what would Spartacus have done with her and her twin if, after he met them, he didn't want them in the tunnels? Would he have trusted them not to say anything if he let them go? They knew enough to damage the operation and Spartacus was practically paranoiac about secrecy.

'You're thinking about what I've said, aren't you?' Bird Girl's eyes were an intense deep grey. 'And you don't really know the answer, do you?'

'Spartacus said he'd lock you up.' Kai tried to make his voice jokey.

Bird Girl shook her head. 'That's what he told me he'd do if I tried to escape when I was underground. Maybe Spartacus said that because he knew that, once I was here, the Cage Fighters wouldn't stand by and let him harm me in any meaningful way. But what I'm asking is, what would Spartacus have done to me had he decided I was untrustworthy and didn't have a good reason for coming underground? What if he'd decided that I was trying to investigate and expose his whole operation?'

Kai shook his head. 'He would have sorted something out.'

Bird Girl dropped her voice to a whisper. 'To keep me silent his solution might have been absolutely awful.'

'No!' Kai replied fiercely. 'Spartacus is not like that. He wouldn't do something bad.' But then he recalled the lock-up. It was very isolated. Anyone held there could have screamed their head off and not been heard. 'I guess he'd just have shut you in the storeroom for the last two days, like he said he would.'

'I suppose that's a relief, then,' Bird Girl said sarcastically. 'Do you think he definitely would have let me have access to water and food and toilet facilities?'

'Yes!' Kai snapped back at her. 'Yes he would. He's very focused on the project, but is basically a kind person. You're suspicious of him because you don't know him.'

Bird Girl looked at Kai searchingly. 'Who *does* know Spartacus?'

CHAPTER TWENTY-FOUR

Kai scraped his chair back and stood up.

'Going to the loo,' he said.

The conversation with Bird Girl had upset him and he needed some thinking time. He wanted to talk about it with Raven but she'd disappeared inside her den followed by Leo. He wouldn't discuss anything like that with Leo present, and he couldn't bear to go there and have to watch Raven applying wild-orange nail varnish to Leo's ridiculous talons.

He went to the toilet and then to his den. His brain was beating like a drum. Spartacus was a good guy – his fault was that sometimes, by the way he acted, he sent out the wrong impressions. He'd done it last night when there had been that mix-up with the photographs on Bird Girl's camera. It seemed as if Spartacus had deliberately deleted them, but actually he'd been working in the background to investigate Bird Girl's story. He'd sent for Mole and was making sure that Mole had enough supplies from the storeroom to keep Dove and the baby birds alive. That was a genuine act of caring. He wasn't a calculating and mean person who only pretended to be nice.

Spartacus was *not* that type of person.

He wasn't.

Kai clenched his fists so hard that his nails dug into his palms.

Evil Eddy *was* that type of person. Worming his way into Kai's mother's heart and her house. Did it so well that his mum stopped believing her own son and took Eddy's word for what was happening when she wasn't there.

Kai tried to tell her that Eddy was lying when he said he spent his days looking for work. Most afternoons, when Kai came in after school Eddy had his friends in drinking and playing computer games. They'd left before Kai's mum got home and Eddy cleared up the mess, but while they were there they expected Kai to fetch and carry for them, make snacks and wash their dirty dishes.

Kai tried bringing his own friends in but that didn't suit Eddy. If they sat in the kitchen, Eddy and his mates would sneer at their clothes, talk over their conversation and disagree with what they said. When Kai took his friends to his room Eddy complained that the music was too loud, even though they were listening with their headphones on. After a while his pals stopped coming round. They couldn't take the constant harassment.

So Kai tried a counterattack. Over several days he took some pics on his phone of the shambles in the living room to show his mum. One evening Kai produced his phone with a flourish: 'Here's what goes on in the house when you're not here, Mum.' He opened his photo file to find it blank.

Eddy relaxed back in his chair. 'You don't mind me having some pals here occasionally, do you, love?' he asked Kai's mum.

Kai was left looking as if he was fabricating stories, saying it was more than 'a few' pals and that they were there most days. Then Eddy smiled at him in a way Kai found more scary than when Eddy was glaring at him.

Later Eddy hoisted Kai up by the collar, half strangling him.

'I always run checks on your phone, you little squirt. Don't think you can outfox me, 'cos you can't. I'll be watching your every move.'

After that, what had been a series of running battles with Eddy became all-out war. The bullying started for real. The armlocks and the knock-about 'let's toughen Kai up a bit' sessions escalated. But, in one way, that had helped Kai. His mum saw a notice in the Community Centre and enrolled him in boxing classes. And so Kai learned to defend himself properly. He began to land professional punches and Eddy couldn't complain.

There were less rough-house sessions but Eddy wasn't a guy to back off. One day Kai came home to find a special model he'd kept from his childhood bent and broken. It was his own design of Treasure Island, based on the description in Robert Louis Stevenson's book, and had sat securely on his bedroom windowsill for years. Now it was lying in pieces on the floor. Kai was stunned.

'Meant to say, I was dusting in here and may have knocked one of your toys over by accident.' Eddy was lounging in the doorway of his room watching his reaction. 'Sorry about that.'

Kai swung round. Eddy's pose altered. His body tensed. His arms hung loose by his side but his hands were balled into fists. His eyes glittered. He was high on something. Whatever it was, Kai knew that it would make Eddy reckless, enough to inflict a bad injury if a fight started.

'Come ahead, wee man,' Eddy said in a sinister voice. 'Time me and you settled once and for all who is king of this castle.'

A coldness descended over Kai's mind and spirit. Eddy intended to pound him to a pulp. He had to keep his head if he was to avoid ending up in Accident and Emergency. Kai held up his hands, palms out. 'You know what? You're right, Eddy. This model *is* a toy.' He picked up the ruined Treasure Island that he'd been so proud of, tossed it into an empty shoe box and rammed it under his bed. He didn't know why *he* should be embarrassed when he'd done nothing wrong, but he didn't want his mum to see the destruction. Eddy would say Kai had smashed it up in a bad temper and his mum would believe him.

And that would be the one thing that Kai couldn't bear. If his mum thought that he'd purposefully break this particular model.

Eddy lingered at the door, unsure how to respond to this change in Kai. 'Don't you worry your mother by running to her and telling tales about me,' he said.

'Nope.' Kai tipped his hand to forehead. 'From now on, Eddy, you're the boss. You're king of the castle.'

The slap was so hard it caught the edge of Kai's teeth.

'Don't you *ever* cheek me again! If you do, there's plenty more where that came from.'

A stale taste on his lips.
Blood.
In his mouth and on his tongue.

That night, before his mother even asked about his split lip, Kai fabricated a story about how he'd been injured in a boxing bout at the Community Centre. As he was lying to his mum there was a greasy smile of approval on Eddy's face.

That was the moment when Kai made the decision to leave home.

He sat on his bed in his den and tried to think why his model being broken was his tipping point. Model-making was something he and his mum had done together when he was smaller. Kai could still feel the thrill of excitement when opening a new pack. Carefully laying out the pieces on the kitchen table.

Mum would spread out a newspaper and he'd work and they'd chat while she prepared dinner. She made suggestions on how Kai could expand the template, the smell from the cooker and the satisfaction of creating an object with his own hands giving him a sense of warm contentment.

Right through his childhood and into his teen years they got along great together – until Evil Eddy arrived.

Mum thought it didn't matter that Eddy wasn't employed at the moment. Eddy said he'd pay his own way. He had savings, he said. From his business that went bust. It was the recession, he said. But he was looking for work. Hopeful that the right job would turn up.

Eddy kept the garden tidy and did some housework and made a dinner of sorts. But the cooker was never on. It was microwave meals and cold ready-prepared pasta, and then more and more takeaway food, which his mum normally paid for.

And he hated Kai and his mum chatting about their time together before he arrived. Once they were sitting watching a programme on the telly about Ernest Shackleton, the famous Antarctic explorer, when his mum said: 'Kai, do you remember the model you made of some island to do with Shackleton? What was it called again?'

'Elephant Island,' said Kai. 'It was where Shackleton's men waited for him to return to rescue them on one of the early polar expeditions when their ship got stuck in the ice.'

'That's right!' Kai's mum laughed. 'I always thought it was a funny name for a frozen place, considering elephants live in hot countries.'

'Parts of the island do look like an elephant. But some people say it got its name because there were elephant seals on it.' Kai smiled at his mum.

'Well, I never knew that.' She disentangled herself from Eddy's arm around her to ruffle Kai's hair. 'You're my best smart lad.'

'What's the matter with you?' Eddie guffawed at Kai. 'Are you some kind of weirdo, sitting here talking to your mummy about making models? Why aren't you in your room like a normal teenager watching YouTube or trawling the Internet?'

Kai wanted to take his Treasure Island model with him when he left, but the shoe box had disappeared from under his bed – Evil Eddy must have flung it out. Kai searched and searched for it, emptying the wheelie bin out over the back garden and examining the rubbish. There wasn't a trace.

He'd had to leave without it.

Kai put his head in his hands. He was reliving the past, and the bad memories surfaced, crowding out the quiet spaces of his mind with their horrible and stomach-griping fears.

'Are you quite well, Kai?'

It was Sarema calling softly to him from outside his den.

Kai stood up, swished his washcloth over his face and opened the door.

'Time for tea?'

Kai managed a smile.

'Do not fall out with Bird Girl, I beg you.' Sarema took his arm as they returned to the café. 'It's difficult for a person to adjust to living down here, especially if it happens suddenly, and you have no choice in the matter. Also Bird Girl has an added anxiety. Although one is happy to do it, caring for one's sister can weigh heavily on the soul.'

As usual, Sarema's observations helped Kai reason things out. Bird Girl was spooked by being underground. It happened to everyone when they first came into the tunnels. It took days to settle in, become accustomed to the enclosed space, the smell of the air and the darkness hovering at the edge of the lit sections. Your senses needed to relearn how to interpret sounds and unsettling sensations you'd never experienced. The elusive vibrations, the muffled thunder of trains far away and the occasional slow change in air pressure as if a giant was turning in its sleep.

'Gita and I have to report to Tech's den for our monitor watching shift,' said Sarema. 'Perhaps you'd like to join us?'

CHAPTER TWENTY-FIVE

'Has Spartacus left HQ?'

Sarema asked Tech the question as the twins took over monitor watch from Boudicca.

Tech nodded. 'He went out to post Magog and Beowulf's fight.'

Sarema smiled at Gita and both girls relaxed in their seats.

'Is Leo in the café?' Boudicca asked them.

'No,' replied Sarema.

'Did you see him around?'

'I couldn't say where he is.' Sarema kept her eyes on the monitor as she fiddled with the brightness control, which Kai thought strange as she must have seen Leo and Raven chatting together.

'Leo's annoying Raven again,' Kai told Boudicca. 'Can't take a hint, that boy.'

'Right!' Boudicca huffed out of the door.

Sarema sighed and looked at Kai ruefully.

'Can't Spartacus post the fights from here?' Bird Girl asked Tech. 'Aren't you linked to the outside world?'

'Too risky,' said Tech. 'The police have very sophisticated tracking equipment. They can discover sources no matter how cleverly they've been covered up.'

'They be not the only ones,' said a voice behind them.

'Mole!' Bird Girl was on her feet and across the room in seconds. 'Did you make the roof safe? Were you in touch with my sister? How is she? How is Dar—' She stopped to correct herself. 'How is Dove?'

'She be happy,' said Mole. 'Roof nearly fixed.'

'Is Dove OK with us running a cable into her den?' asked Kai.

'Did she write a note?' Bird Girl was in a nervous fever. 'What did she say?'

Mole squinted his eyes around the room to see who was there. Then he took a piece of paper from his pocket and gave it to Bird Girl.

'Would you read it out to us?' said Sarema.

Bird Girl scanned the page and then began to read aloud:

Albert has bread for birds. Albert want to bring a movie camera so ye can talk to me

If Albert is the White Rat then what is your name?

I be Mole

Do you live down here?

I do

Aren't you afraid of the dark?

I don't be afraid of dark

Me neither but most other people are.

They be not smart

Thank you for the bread. Albert can bring a movie camera.

'When will you take the camera to her?' Bird Girl asked in anxiety.

'Later.' Mole put his palms together and laid his hands flat alongside his cheek and closed his eyes. 'She sleep now.'

'I hate to think of her alone and in the dark.'

'She has torch and she be not alone.' Mole tapped his top pocket, which was empty. 'Albert be there.'

'You left Albert with her?' Bird Girl's eyes filled with tears. 'You are so kind. I appreciate how much Albert means to you.'

'I've got the stuff ready for you, Mole.' Tech pointed to the bag containing the audio-visual cables and camera.

'It's a pity we don't have more time to bring down the other equipment.' Kai thought of the boxes in the lock-up. 'Spartacus has got the new digging tools you asked for, Mole.'

Mole looked at Kai. 'Don't ask for no digging tools,' he said. 'Too noisy. Not so safe.'

'If you don't use digging tools then how do you get through blocked-off routes?' asked Bird Girl. 'How will you eventually rescue my sister?'

'Dig with hands.' Mole held them up. His nails were ragged and his hands and fingers heavily calloused and ingrained with dirt. 'Maybe Spartacus be lookin' for his own pot o' gold.'

'What do you mean by that? Is Spartacus doing something else in the tunnels as well as setting up the cage fights?' Bird Girl moved nearer to Mole to ask him this.

Mole looked at her. He extended two fingers so that their tips rested above Bird Girl's eyebrows. 'You see a lot,' he said. He waved at Kai and the rest of the people in the room. 'More than they see.'

'I'm here for one reason,' said Bird Girl. 'To rescue my sister.'

Mole went very close to Bird Girl and peered into her face. He seemed satisfied with what he saw there. 'You got shiny hair.' Mole lifted a strand. 'Like gold it be.' He let it drop. 'Golden treasure.' He glanced at Kai. 'There be all kinds of treasure for a body to find if only they do see it.' He picked up the carrier bag and left.

'If the Meet's early today I'd better get some training in before Spartacus comes back,' said Kai.

Bird Girl walked with him to the door. 'I'm sorry if what I say about Spartacus upsets you, but he's not as open as the rest of you guys,' she stated flatly. 'Do you really believe that his sole purpose in being here is to help young people make some money to get a new start in life?'

'He let us know from the beginning that he was in it for himself too,' said Kai. 'He told us he needed to make money to live. His disability was reassessed and his benefits cut. The allowance he gets means he can barely survive, or keep warm in the winter.'

'I know about benefit cuts and restrictions,' said Bird Girl. 'There's loads of people living like that now. Having to make a choice between eating and keeping warm.'

'His mum died and they took his two-bedroom Council flat away from him. Said they'd move him fifty miles outside London. Had to think up a way to get some cash so he could stay near his friends and support groups.'

'Yeah, but' – Bird Girl waved her arm around – 'why this in particular?'

'Before he was injured he was into boxing, was about to go professional, so he knows how to train and organize us. And with his leg the way it is, then there's not much else he can do.'

'There's something out of sync though,' said Bird Girl. 'You guys don't see it because you feel beholden to him for rescuing you. The Cage Fighters treat him the same way Sarema treats you, Kai. Like a god-creature.'

Kai burst out laughing. He stretched out his arms and flexed his muscles. 'Hey! I'm a god! Superhero me!'

Bird Girl joined in his laughter and thumped her fist heavily on his arm. Kai pushed instinctively at her hand. And suddenly he was conscious of the softness of her skin, of how near she was to him and the deepening darkness of her eyes . . .

'I – I,' she stammered and they sprang apart. 'Sorry,' she said. 'Didn't mean to punch you so hard, actually.'

'No harm done,' replied Kai, but his voice wasn't quite steady. He waited, making no attempt to move further away.

Neither did she . . .

And then the moment was shattered by an exclamation from Sarema.

'Look!' she cried out. 'The rats are running!'

CHAPTER TWENTY-SIX

'Rats constantly move about underground.' Tech swivelled his chair to get a better look. 'We've seen them before.'

'More than usual.' Sarema indicated a monitor. A dozen rats were running along one of the tunnels.

'Let me see!' Bird Girl crossed the room.

'The rats are nowhere near the old Langsdaine Station,' Sarema reassured her.

'Are they heading this way?' asked Kai.

'No.' Tech checked Sarema's monitor and then the other screens. 'They're moving in the opposite direction. Running away from us.' He frowned. 'I've never seen such a large number on the move before.'

'It's like that Pied Piper poem we read in school.' Kai stared, fascinated, at the screen. '*And out of the houses the rats came tumbling . . .*'

'There are a number of rivers under London,' said Tech. 'If there's been much rain recently then the water levels have probably risen and flooded their nests.'

'It's been raining heavily off and on for days and days,' said Bird Girl. 'Being down here means you don't have any idea what the weather is like on the surface.'

'You're right,' said Tech. 'I noticed Raven was drenched when she came back in yesterday with your phone. Had to give her my towel to dry her hair.'

'Will this affect the last two cage fights?' asked Bird Girl.

'Shouldn't do,' said Kai. 'But Spartacus will decide when he gets back in.'

'Only one day to go and then it's over,' said Tech. 'I've enjoyed the filming, but I'll be glad to get out of here.'

'Have you made plans?' Kai became curious. The nature of Tech's work mostly kept him separate from the others and Kai only knew the outline of his story.

'Yeah, I've made plans.' Tech busied himself at his desk.

'Uh, OK,' said Kai. 'See you guys later at the Meet.'

Sarema and Gita waved in response, as did Bird Girl, but her eyes were on the screen, which still showed the moving pack of rats.

The monitor screens were blank when Spartacus returned. He was unconcerned when Tech told him about the rats.

'They'll head towards the Thames,' he said. 'They

know that's the main food source. Nothing for us to worry about.'

Spartacus knew why the rats were running.

It wasn't heavy rain filling the gulleys and drains to sweep away their nests.

It was because he, Spartacus, had put in place the last part of his scheme.

Fetching the boxes of explosives from the lock-up and hiding them in certain wall cavities had disturbed the creatures. Animals had an instinct for survival. Some primeval sense had warned the rats that death was in the air and they must move on.

Spartacus was aware that the unity of the group was fracturing. In order to keep the Cage Fighters settled he'd crammed the final bouts into the last few days. But the ones who'd been put out were bored. Modern youngsters were spoiled – they'd no discipline, no staying power. Their rebelliousness would have happened anyway, even without the arrival of Bird Girl. She was a major complication. But in one way, that had turned out to be useful. It meant he knew exactly where Mole was. Instead of sneaking about spying on them, the skinny freak was occupied getting that repulsive rat of his to run back and forth with messages and setting up the camera and microphone.

Spartacus allowed himself a smile. After being forced to leave the army, his life was beginning to look up again. He'd felt utterly patronized at being asked to help out for free in a grotty little gym. He was convinced that the teenagers laughed at him behind his back, mocking him and how he limped. If it hadn't been for that accident, which – despite what his superior officer said – was *not* his own fault, he'd have been a championship boxer and wouldn't have to waste his time with these no-hopers.

In the gym he met that sanctimonious do-gooder Tech, drivelling on about his drug-addict sister who'd died alone on the street, and how his dream was to make a tribute film as her memorial. The kids were a mixed bunch, and the gym ran programmes of instruction in boxing or judo or karate. Tech suggested staging a tournament – boxing combined with martial arts – to give them something to aim for. He wanted to build a closed cage with bars to indicate how young rough sleepers were trapped in real life.

Spartacus saw instantly that there was money to be made.

Lots of money.

He subscribed to the Mixed Martial Arts websites and had enough Internet savvy to recognize the idea's potential. He offered to invest in Tech's film as a pay-per-view project to raise money for homeless charities and give the kids a bonus too. 'We'll open secure accounts for the deposits,' he told Tech. 'In your name, of course.' During days of smooth talking he persuaded Tech that it would work better being secret.

'Adds an extra buzz for interest and it's too much hassle to get a licence and comply with official Rules and Regs. We'll make our own. To give it a lift I'll scout the squats for a couple of more experienced fighters. Organize the whole project as a quick hit. Get them to commit to a month, maybe more. If it flops, then no harm done. If it takes off, at the end we do a big "reveal" for the media. Masses of publicity. Highlights the whole vulnerable-homeless-youth situation,' Spartacus added. 'Might even shame the Government into doing something concrete.'

It was the last sentence that had brought Tech round to his way of thinking. 'If we're doing it off the record, where could we stage it so we're not interrupted or stopped halfway through?' Tech had asked him.

Spartacus had already thought where to stage it. He'd kept an old lock-up from the days when he could afford a car. Had been thinking of living there since he got notice to quit his accommodation. One night he'd turned a corner in a street near the lock-up to see a head pop up from a manhole cover and then disappear. The next morning, armed with an industrial torch, he went exploring.

And found the mad lad called Mole.

Spartacus made it his business to befriend Mole, using his savings to buy him food and water and treats for his pet rat. Watching Mole go about underground taught him where the tunnels intersected and how to discover secret accesses.

In exchange for an endless supply of materials, Mole had said he'd help with the project. It meant that Spartacus was able to establish a base for the tournament and gain intimate knowledge of the network of tunnels.

It also meant that he knew exactly where to set explosive charges to seal off the exits. Tomorrow night he planned to walk free while all of them would be trapped – caged in the darkness of the underground tunnels.

CHAPTER
TWENTY-SEVEN

His conversation with Raven about her name must have had some effect, for, to Kai's surprise, she chose to sit beside him at the Meet.

Spartacus gave her a stern look when she came into Tech's den, late as always. Kai was never sure whether Raven, who didn't wear a watch, wasn't conscious of the time or if her arrival was by way of a statement to show that she wouldn't be bossed around by anyone.

'Soz.' Raven flapped her hand at Spartacus, took one of the stacking stools and placed it alongside Kai.

'Well, now that everyone is here . . .' Spartacus rustled some sheets of paper.

Kai tried to concentrate as Spartacus droned on, but it was mainly the usual info relating to food and toilets and conduct and noise levels. Some updates on the state of the tunnels. More warnings and rules and then Spartacus handed each of the Fighters a single sheet of paper.

'This is the final schedule and wind-down arrangements. Study it, and if there's something you don't under-stand or anything is bothering you, please let me know.' He looked at the twins. 'As Kai brought you here then he will take you topside but I suppose you had better have a copy too, so that you know what's happening.' He paused. He knew that the Cage Fighters liked the girls. The twins kept out of people's way and were helpful. It would be best to acknowledge this. Another aid to keeping everyone on-side as the stress increased over the next forty-eight hours. Spartacus cleared his throat. 'I will give Sarema and Gita one hundred pounds each. This will come from my share. But' – he spoke directly to Sarema – 'instead of trying to live on your own again, you should go to a women's refuge. Bear in mind that you might have died had we not rescued you. So please do not betray us by giving any information whatsoever about the Cage Fighters or the tunnels to the authorities.'

Sarema stood up to take the sheet of paper from Spartacus. She made a small bow to him. 'My twin and I say thank you. We will not betray you.' She bowed to the whole group. 'Again we say, thank you.' There was a scattering of applause as she sat down.

Spartacus looked at Bird Girl and then at the door. 'I'd

asked Mole to report back at this time to tell me what's happening at Langsdaine.'

Bird Girl looked apprehensive. She didn't want to tell Spartacus that Mole hadn't waited for him but had instead given them his update. 'I—' she began.

'Mole came by while you were out,' said Kai. 'Was in a hurry though.'

'Yeah,' Tech backed him up. 'Said he'd almost sorted the roof and that Dove was sleeping so he'd try to set the camera up tomorrow morning.'

There was a silence. Kai held his breath, anticipating an angry reaction from Spartacus.

'Does he intend to stay there until that work is finished?' Spartacus asked.

Tech nodded.

'Until tomorrow?'

'He reassured me that he'd not leave Dove on her own.'

'Very good.' Far from annoying Spartacus their answers seemed to please him. 'I knew he was the lad for the job.' He smiled at Bird Girl. 'After Leo and Kai fight tomorrow we'll see if we can get a visual on your sister. Now Raven and Boudicca should get into costume for their epic battle.' He grinned at the girls. 'I'm really looking forward to this – our first finalists of the tournament!'

Kai was *not* looking forward to Raven fighting Boudicca. Spartacus had said he would speak to both fighters about the boundaries before each match, but in Magog and Beowulf's fight no clear lines had been drawn. Kai decided he wouldn't go to the Arena and watch them in action. Instead he went to his den, lay down on his bed and put in his ear buds.

Boudicca had the same build as Leo and was the same brand of fighter, using height and weight and deviousness to outfox a more resourceful opponent. Raven was wiry and tough, but there was no guarantee that she would overpower Boudicca. They were each on form and up for it, but Kai worried that Boudicca might have the crucial edge. He couldn't bear to see Raven being defeated.

He closed his eyes and blanked his mind as to what was happening in the Cage.

When he awoke Kai went to Tech's den to find out the result. As he entered Tech was shovelling things haphazardly about his desk.

'You OK?' Kai asked.

Tech shook his head.

'A nasty fight in the Cage,' Magog said from his seat at the monitor. 'Worse than mine. That was not a nice end to the girls' competition.'

'What's up?' Kai asked, then his heart hiccupped and he said, 'Did Raven lose out to Boudicca in the Cage?'

'No,' Tech answered abruptly. 'Raven won the contest. If you can call that winning.'

'What do you mean? Is Boudicca OK?'

'Boudicca is fine. She was outclassed and played some rotten tricks – especially at the end.'

'Raven got hurt?' The look on Tech's face told Kai the answer. 'How bad?'

'She wouldn't let me tend to her. Before Spartacus went out to post their fight he gave Sarema the full first-aid kit from the storeroom. She and Bird Girl are with her now.'

Kai was gone before Tech finished speaking.

Raven was lying on her bed with Sarema and Bird Girl kneeling beside her. There were bruises rising below her eyes and her face was marked with scratches and tears.

'The fight was very unpleasant,' Sarema said as Kai entered. 'Boudicca was in a bad temper.'

Raven sat up. 'I don't want you fussing over me,' she told him. 'In fact, all of you can beat it. I'm going to sleep for a few hours.'

'Perhaps I should put on more antiseptic ointment and—' Sarema began.

'Shut the door on your way out,' snapped Raven.

Kai, understanding that Raven's self-respect was connected to her not breaking down, quickly ushered Sarema and Bird Girl ahead of him and closed the door of Raven's den, leaving her alone.

'What happened?' he asked the other two girls.

'Spartacus discussed relaxing the rules,' Sarema told him. 'He said it would make the fight more interesting. Boudicca was keen but Raven refused. Boudicca was furious and lashed out from the beginning.'

'Raven kept cool and gained most points in the first

two rounds,' said Bird Girl. 'Then, in round three, Boudicca pulled Raven's face visor up. Claimed afterwards that it was an accident, but—'

'You think Boudicca did it deliberately? I know she's hot-headed, but why would she do that?'

'Kai.' Sarema gave her head a shake. 'Sometimes you do not see what is happening close to you. Boudicca likes Leo. Leo pays Raven the attention Boudicca wants. I don't think Boudicca cared about losing the fight, as long as she hurt Raven.'

'Things are turning sour,' said Kai. 'I'll be glad to get into the Cage tomorrow and get this tournament over.'

Sarema laid her hand on Kai's arm. 'Be careful,' she said. 'Be very careful.'

CHAPTER TWENTY-EIGHT

The following morning the Cage Fighters were in a mood of high excitement.

Everyone had been told to report to the café at 10 a.m. on the final fight day. To a welcoming noise of whoops and shouts of laughter, Spartacus came there waving a bank statement and a bundle of banknotes in the air.

'My great announcement is that we've made much more than I anticipated!'

'How much?' Leo called out. And his question was taken up by the others until it became a chant:

'How much? How much? How much?'

'Tech will calculate the percentages but at least a thousand more each.'

'Hallelujah!' Magog put his hands around Medusa's waist and lifted her off her feet.

The rest of the Cage Fighters clapped and began hugging each other.

Spartacus held up his hand for silence. 'Here's the plan for the day. This morning you pack your gear for leaving. At noon we stage the final fight – the one between Leo and Kai. For this I want total commitment. Everyone is to be there to cheer them on. This will be mega as regards future pay-offs. More atmosphere means more interest, which builds up the Internet chatter leading to more viewers. So, even more money for you guys *and* donations to help all those homeless kids sleeping rough. So clap, boo, hooray and hoot your heads off. To big up the noise, Tech's going to play audience sound effects from professional games during this match.

'Also Tech's going to do an instant edit on this, our very last film, so that I can get it on our website ASAP. Afternoon will be spent clearing up. We may want to use this place again so let's make it tidy. Finish packing your rucksacks and try to get some rest. I'll be back in the evening when I've withdrawn the rest of the money for your initial payments – but don't worry; the bulk of it is already sitting happily in the safe in the storeroom! I just want to collect the latest deposits, because these will be larger amounts. This evening is when I'll portion it out. As agreed, each person gets the same basic rate for every fight fought. The runners-up earn more and, of course, the winners get top bonus.'

Leo pointed to his own chest as if to say: 'That's me!'

'In your dreams!' said Kai. He smacked one fist into his opposite palm. 'I'll grind your bones to dust!'

'You're dog meat!' Leo answered.

Kai snorted and looked around for Bird Girl. She was standing in a corner with Sarema and Gita. Her hair was matted and her eyes heavy as if she hadn't had much sleep.

Kai made his way to her and the twins. 'Any news?'

'Mole dropped in to say he'll be sending Albert back and forth with cable now,' said Bird Girl. 'Tech might have it working before he has to film the fight. He said he'd come and tell me when it went live.'

'That's good,' said Kai. 'Isn't it?' he added as the girls didn't respond.

'Spartacus ordered that everyone must be in the Arena to watch your fight,' said Sarema. 'We are concerned at the change of routine. There will be no one looking at the monitors.'

'That was explained in the handout,' said Kai. 'Normally Tech adds sound effects but Spartacus thinks it would be better to have the noise of a live audience too for the last fight. Also he wants Tech to do mini interviews with the other Cage Fighters during the breaks between rounds. It'll help build the viewing hits, which means more money.'

'How long will you stay after the fight is over?' asked Bird Girl.

'Most of us have our rucksacks packed already but as Spartacus just said, we wait until the share-out. I reckon we'll be going out about midnight tonight.'

'What about me?'

'I'll take you as well as the twins,' said Kai. 'Mole is bound to have made contact with your sister by then. If he can't dig through there by tonight so that she can come topside with us, you can go straight to the police and tell them where Dove is hiding.'

'I don't want to tell the police where Dove is hiding,' said Bird Girl. 'If my sister says that she'll run away again and hide in a deeper tunnel if she's forced to leave the birds, then that's exactly what she'll do.'

Kai's mouth fell open. 'Are you thinking of staying here until the chicks can fly?'

Bird Girl set her chin. 'Yes, if that's what it takes to make her safe.'

'I don't think Spartacus will be happy with that,' said Kai. 'I'm not sure whether he intends to wait on or return to take the furniture topside, but I don't think he'll say yes to you staying on.'

'I'm not going to tell him,' said Bird Girl. 'I'll speak to Mole.'

Kai glanced towards Spartacus, who was surrounded by excited Cage Fighters. 'Wait until the fight is over and I can be with you when you ask him. Mole and I get along quite well.'

*

Kai's mind was on Bird Girl as he went to his den to put his belongings in his rucksack. He wasn't happy that she'd be alone in the tunnels with only Mole for company. It wasn't that Mole was dangerous; he was bizarre – no doubt about that – but he was harmless. It was more the thought of Bird Girl being here on her own.

And . . . Spartacus would be bound to find out. How would he react when he discovered Bird Girl still here after everyone else had left? What would he do?

Kai considered taking Sarema and Gita topside and then coming back and staying with Bird Girl until Dove was ready to come out of her den. It was only when he'd finished packing that Kai realized with a jolt that, in all the options he was considering, he hadn't once thought about Raven.

Spartacus watched them with amusement as they took their seats in the Arena for the final fight to begin. They were exchanging phone numbers and telling each other what they were going to do with their money.

Idiots! Did they really think he'd invest his savings in some silly project for kids who couldn't face up to life? Did they think that they were entitled to have part of the profits when it was he who had paid for their costumes, equipment and food? He'd waved the banknotes about in order to keep them motivated – but there would be no cash share-out for any of them. The attitude of young people angered him beyond belief. He thought back to the hardship of his own youth. Although the army had been beneficial because of the boxing training, he was always on report for some transgression or other. It riled him when younger recruits were promoted above him and he had to obey their instructions. One day, on active service, he'd ignored orders. Two fellow soldiers had been killed and he was badly injured. They'd offered him a way out, avoiding an investigation. Bile rose from his stomach as he recalled his humiliation. But that was in the past. With the money he'd make on this he was on the way up.

No doubt alarms would ring when he set off his explosives, but he'd also call the emergency services and give them the location of the underground HQ. He'd say there were tunnel cave-ins and they'd need equipment to get the teenagers out. He'd send a message too, about the girl holed up at the old Langsdaine Station. He wouldn't *deliberately* leave anyone to die . . . but being really imprisoned for a while might teach them a lesson.

And these gullible youths wouldn't be left with nothing. They'd likely make some cash from newspaper interviews, or get on a TV reality show. Kai lacked raw ruthlessness, but Boudicca, Leo, Beowulf, and maybe even Raven could earn a living from official cage fighting.

Spartacus beckoned to Kai and Leo.

'I need a word with you guys,' he said. He drew them to one side. 'This is a private talk – not to be discussed with anyone else at any point, now or in the future. Got that?'

'Fine,' Leo agreed.

After a moment Kai nodded.

'There's a way that the two of you could make even more money, like *a lot* more money from this last bout. We'd need to spin it out, add four more rounds to maximize the drama. It's a big ask, but I'm talking about big amounts. A sure-fire six grand each. Probably more.'

'What do we have to do?' asked Leo.

'Make the fight last as long as possible,' said Spartacus. 'We'll announce it as a seven-round match fight instead of three. Both of you must agree to let each other win alternate rounds until you reach round five. Kai, you win rounds one and three, then Leo, you win rounds two and four. After that, it's no holds barred. There's no points to be scored. It's the last man standing who wins.'

'For six grand I'm in!' said Leo.

'Kai?'

'I guess so,' Kai said slowly.

'Terrific!' Spartacus pretended not to notice Kai's hesitation. 'Now, the bank told me this morning that I can't wait until this evening to make such a large withdrawal – I have to go in there personally this afternoon. So I need to go topside ASAP to get the rest of the money. Tech will act as your judge. I'll do the intros but won't be around until after the fight. Then we'll all be together for the share-out!'

'We'd have no referee?' Kai asked.

'Exactly!' Spartacus nodded enthusiastically.

'No restrictions on what we do?' There was an expression on Leo's face – the same look Kai had sometimes seen on Evil Eddy's.

'That's it!' Again Spartacus brimmed with enthusiasm. 'No holds barred. No rules.'

'Not even the basics?' asked Kai. 'You mean we can go ahead with biting and eye-gouging?'

'I'm relying on your own decency,' said Spartacus. He checked his watch. 'We'd better get started. Tech will film it as usual and I'll put Raven on the bell.'

'Is Raven fit enough?' asked Kai.

'She's looking forward to it.'

Kai looked around. 'Where is she?'

'Helping Tech,' Spartacus replied.

'I thought she'd be here to wish me luck for the fight,' said Leo.

'To wish *me* luck for the fight,' said Kai.

'She's totally bored with you, Brainbox Boy. It's pathetic the way you hang around her at every opportunity.'

'You're the one's that pathetic. Raven only tolerates you 'cos she feels sorry for you!'

Spartacus was glad to hear that Kai and Leo's rivalry over the girl still fuelled their mutual dislike. He'd fretted that the arrival of Bird Girl would have diverted or diluted their aggro. 'Didn't I see her with you earlier?' he asked Leo. It wasn't true, but he knew Leo wouldn't say that. And putting the thought in Kai's head would needle him. He'd orchestrated their dislike of each other from the moment they met. Interrupting their first handshake to set them at loggerheads. Of the group they were the two best fighters. The only ones with sparkle. If he wanted to make money then he needed to make them dislike each other on a personal basis so that they'd be wilder in the Cage. And he'd worked so hard on it – seeding bad-tempered reactions in both of them with remarks and comments, while pretending to favour each one individually. Giving them fighting tips, especially Leo, who needed an edge to keep up with Kai. For this last fight he wanted to bring their anger to the boil so they'd be too hot-headed to question his suggestions.

'I'm sure Raven will be along to wish both of you good luck.' Sarema had appeared at Spartacus's elbow. 'She is feeling so much better.'

Spartacus tutted at her for defusing the situation. 'Just remember, each and every person who is underground has to be in the Arena within five minutes.'

'There's Raven now,' said Leo.

Before Kai could move Leo had gone to greet Raven, who was coming into the Arena with Tech.

'Has Mole returned? Is the camera set up?' Bird Girl joined them.

Tech shook his head. 'Mole reported back to say that what he has to do will take longer. At least an hour or more.'

As Bird Girl's shoulders slumped in disappointment

Spartacus's spirits soared. This was perfect. An hour plus was enough time for him to empty the safe in the storeroom, set the explosives and get topside to clean out the bank accounts.

He looked at Kai and Leo.

'All set?' he asked them.

'All set,' they replied.

CHAPTER TWENTY-NINE

Tech turned off the main lights.

A single spot lit the Cage from above.

Spartacus bellowed through his megaphone: 'And now! The final you've all been waiting for! The last match in our extraordinary *Cage Fighters for Freedom* tournament!

'First in the Cage is the King of the Jungle. The mighty Leo!'

To the sound of African music and roaring lions Leo strutted into the Cage. He dropped down on all fours and prowled about, pawing at the bars. The watching Cage Fighters clapped and stamped. Tech switched on his backup tape and the volume of noise magnified.

With a roar Leo leaped to his feet and clawed at the air. His painted nails caught the spotlight and flashed wild-orange. There was the crack of a whip. Once. Twice.

Tossing his head from side to side and still roaring, Leo backed into his corner.

'And now!' Spartacus spoke again and the Arena quietened. 'The unquenchable flame! We present Kai! The Fire within a Firestorm!'

The low crackling noise of a burning bonfire rapidly rose to become the monstrous rushing rage of a forest fire. Kai imagined how he'd appear on film – the pulsating flames of his helmet, the carmine red of his fight vest. He stepped up and into the Cage.

'I'll tear you to pieces with my talons!' Leo curled his fingers and clawed the air.

Kai turned his back on him. He punched his fists in the air three times, crossed his arms over his chest and spun right round to face Leo.

'I'll trap you in a circle of fire!' he cried.

'Prepare to bleed!' yelled Leo.

'Prepare to burn!' yelled Kai.

Suddenly the whole Cage juddered, bucking them both to their knees. The floor rocked and then steadied.

Kai was first on his feet. 'What happened?'

'Jeez-oh!' Leo got up. 'Was that an earthquake?'

'The earthquake is *here!*' Spartacus's voice brayed from the darkness. 'For this last fight the Cage has been raised from the floor! Hanging free! With no referee! Suspended from a steel cable. An extra challenge for our championship challengers. A surprise for you! And – as you can see – a surprise for our Cage Fighters too! But no surprise for anyone when I say this is the best fight of the tournament! The final play-off! Can the King of the Jungle quench the Flame of Flames? Or will the Firestorm incinerate the Leader of the Pride?

'Leo or Kai?

'Kai or Leo?

'Let's hear it for Leo!

'Let's hear it for Kai!'

As the howling response faded Spartacus went on, 'And, to add to the excitement, we've made this fight special in another way.

'Will it be three rounds?

'No!

'Five rounds?

'No!

'For tonight only! In this last match in the *Cage Fighters for Freedom* tournament, Leo and Kai will fight for seven – I'll say that again – for *seven* rounds.

'A seven-round "no holds barred" match!

'Yes, folks! This match between Leo and Kai tonight is a "Kill Fight".

'Good luck, Cage Fighters!

'Let the games begin!'

Spartacus banged his megaphone on the bars, causing the Cage to swing from side to side.

The bell rang.

Leo had put on his gloves and he launched himself at Kai, raining punches on his chest.

Kai seized him in a neck lock. 'Listen, thicko. I'm supposed to win the first round! Remember?'

'Had to do that,' said Leo. 'To show that you're not as fast as you think you are.'

Kai whacked him on the head with the side of his fist. Leo went down. Kai danced around as Leo faked getting up, collapsed back onto the floor, and repeated the whole procedure until the bell rang for the end of the round.

Kai went to his corner. Somebody shoved a stool, a towel and bucket of water through the bars. The spot gave enough light for Kai to see Tech interviewing Raven for her opinion on the fight. Then he moved to Boudicca and Magog. The Cage Fighters were dressed in their costumes, hair covered and faces masked by their helmets and visors. Kai couldn't locate Sarema or Gita or Bird Girl. They must be sitting at the back. And, of course, Spartacus himself was gone.

When the bell went for Round Two Leo came out of his corner in supreme confidence. Kai regretted that he'd agreed to cave in to him. Leo would maximize his lion act, secure in the knowledge that Kai had to let him win this round. Several times Kai thought he could have bested him with a good punch but had to let it go. Eventually Leo put a semi-wrestle hold on Kai, who conceded a submission.

Rounds Three and Four followed the same pattern. Leo reacted to an early blow from Kai in Round Three by playing groggy until the bell rang. When Round Four came and it was his turn to win, he posed about for even longer, growling and pulling his gloves off and on to display his curved claws, leaving Kai frustrated and getting angrier and angrier.

Now it was Round Five and it really would be 'no holds barred'.

The memory of their last fight was in Kai's head. He was going to keep his eyes on Leo and not be fooled again. Leo's energy was running high. He'd used Kai's winning rounds to save his strength. But his superiority was in his height and weight. Kai dodged and ducked, more skilful and nimble on his feet. Counting the seconds in his head.

Ten to go.

Kai went blazing into the attack and struck. A massive undercut to the jaw. And Leo was on the floor as the bell rang to end the round.

Kai jumped across Leo and raised both hands in the air so that there was no doubt as to who had won that round.

The din of sound from outside the Cage increased as Round Six began. Tech must have turned up the audio track. As if on cue Leo rocketed forward in a flurry of punches. Kai hunched his back and used his fists to defend himself, whereupon Leo crouched and kicked out malevolently at Kai's shins. It was so unexpected that Kai stumbled. He felt his ankle give under him and he went over. He stayed down. Best to let this round go. The bell rang. As Kai got up to go to his corner Leo thumped him hard with both fists on the top of his helmet.

No referee to declare him out.

Kai staggered to his stool. His vision was blurred, his hearing fuzzy. The noise became a sound like the sea surging against rocks. The way it does around an island . . . lines of foam creaming on the sand . . . Kai gave his head a shake – some part of his brain acknowledging that he might be concussed. Through glazed eyes he saw Tech interviewing Beowulf. Raven seemed to be slow to ring the bell for the last round. Spartacus had probably also asked her to make the fight last longer so that every Cage Fighter could comment – Tech wanted them to make individual statements on the hardship and hazards of life on the street. But maybe it was to give Spartacus more time to bring their money back in.

Tech finished his interview and turned up his sound track. Bass notes of drumbeats throbbed in the air.

Kai's ears were buzzing. The level of noise was so much louder. Like club music fully amped up on speakers.

The speakers . . .

There was something about the speakers. Kai tried to think. From the beginning two enormous speakers had sat beside the Cage. They'd never been used because Spartacus was neurotic about noise. When listening to their own music the Cage Fighters used ear buds or headphones, Spartacus ever anxious that any unusual sound would be picked up by Underground staff and reported.

Until this fight.

Why? This was their championship finale. The last pay-off, a mega amount riding on this one. That's what Spartacus had said. He wanted to big it up. But why so much noise? Why take this risk when Tech could add it in later as he generally did? Yet it must always have been Spartacus's intention to use the speakers, otherwise he would not have set them up . . .

The bell clanged.

Last round.

Kai got up.

Leo was coming towards him.

Slowly.

Kai took a single step forward, allowing himself more time to recover from the blow to the top of his head at the end of the previous round.

Leo waited . . . watching. Like a lion with its wounded prey.

Kai tottered. Unsure.

Wild-orange claws scratched at his arm.

'Said I'd make you bleed,' Leo snarled.

Kai stared stupidly as the red welts oozed blood. Leo had taken a glove off! His nails were filed razor-sharp.

'That's a foul!' yelled Kai.

'It's a "Kill Fight"!' Leo yelled back. 'Anyway Spartacus told me to do it.'

'Spartacus told you to make that move on me?' Kai repeated in disbelief.

'That, and a few others,' Leo smirked.

'Like mash my head after the bell?'

Leo nodded. Sweat was pouring down his neck. He was high on the prospect of an imminent win.

Images swam through Kai's mind. Was Bird Girl right? Had Spartacus been manipulating them all along?

'We need to stop – to talk!' he called out to Leo.

'No way!' cried Leo. 'Spartacus warned me you might pull a trick like this – use some excuse to stop the fight.'

'Spartacus warned *you* against *me*?'

'Yeah. From when we first met.' Leo advanced as he was speaking. 'He told me what a liar you are, always talking about people behind their backs.'

'Spartacus warned me about *you*!' Kai jumped to avoid Leo's spinning side-kick. 'Said Raven wasn't safe in your company.'

'That's garbage! Spartacus is my friend. He'd never say anything like that about me.' Now Leo was close enough to try a head-butt.

Kai retreated quickly. His back was against the Cage bars. Fists up. Kicking out to defend himself. Leo was right. Spartacus had never *actually* said that. Just implied it, with remarks and gestures.

'Liar! Liar! Liar!' Gloves back on, Leo was pummelling Kai's arms and body.

'You're angry because you know it's true!' Kai shouted.

'But there is something wrong with the set-up for this fight!'

'The only thing that's wrong for you is that you're going to lose.' Leo was beyond listening.

'It's too noisy out there!' Kai reached out both hands and grabbed Leo's head. 'The vibrations must be travelling right through the tunnels. Spartacus would know that might be heard by railway workers.'

'Don't be daft.' Leo broke free. 'He wouldn't risk wrecking the project.'

'Maybe he doesn't care.' Kai moved aside as Leo came towards him in full fight mode. 'Maybe he's made enough money already and has bailed on us.'

'There's tons more to make on this fight.' Leo's foot shot out but failed to connect. 'Probably more than all the others put together.'

'Bird Girl thinks he manipulates us, that he's just in this for himself.'

'Bird Girl. Bird Girl.' Leo mimicked Kai's voice. 'She's really got you fooled, hasn't she?'

'What she says makes sense. Think about it, please, Leo,' Kai begged.

For answer Leo took off both gloves, lunged forwards and raked his nails along Kai's neck.

Kai knew the cuts were deep, felt himself sliding into shock. Losing his thoughts amid the sound booming beyond the cage, blocking every sense.

Suddenly one noise above the rest. A sound unlike

any other Kai had ever heard. A gigantic underground door slamming shut.

A tremendous thud and a whoosh of air.

The Cage jerked and spun.

The two fighters swayed between dark and light as the Cage wobbled.

Above the pounding drums came a high-pitched shriek.

Leo stopped in mid-punch, his hands poised in the air.

The music shut off.

Empty silence.

Then – a piercing scream of terror. And another, and another.

'What's happening?' Kai flung himself at the bars, trying to see into the blackness.

Leo swung himself to the roof of the Cage. He shoved his arm through the spars and pulled at the electric cable. The spotlight swivelled so that it shone onto the surrounding area where the audience had been sitting to watch this last match.

People were climbing onto their chairs, clutching each other and shouting. The floor was alive with an undulating stream of movement.

Rats.

Hundreds upon hundreds of rats, huge and horrible, eyes gleaming red, were swarming everywhere.

CHAPTER THIRTY

A shout from Leo.

Kai looked up. A rat had scrabbled down the cable and onto Leo's arm. He shook it off and the animal dropped to the floor. It ran around the cage and then leaped out between the bars.

'Jeez-oh!' Leo shouted. 'We need to get out of the Cage!'

'Can we call this fight quits then?' said Kai.

'OK,' Leo replied. Then added, 'It's a no-win.'

'Whatever.' Kai was already at the Cage door. And there were Sarema and Bird Girl, who had manoeuvred their chairs across the floor.

'I must go to my sister!' Bird Girl called to Kai.

Kai helped her and Sarema up and into the Cage. Below them, squeaking and squealing, the rats raced on. 'Do we know what caused that bang?' he asked them.

'A tunnel cave-in?' suggested Leo.

'I do not think so,' said Sarema. 'From where we were at the back it sounded more like explosions.'

'*Explosions!*' Kai exclaimed. 'You mean there was more than one?'

'We're not sure,' said Bird Girl.

'And Spartacus is not here for us to ask him what it could be and what we should do,' said Sarema.

Kai searched for an explanation. Sarema had mentioned Spartacus's name . . . 'You think Spartacus—'

'We need to do our emergency evacuation,' Leo called to Tech, who was poised on a chair, still filming. 'Can you switch the main lights on?'

Tech pointed to the ground. 'I'm not budging until these guys have gone through.'

'I can't go without Darcey!' Bird Girl put her hands on Kai's chest. 'Can you help me find my sister?'

Kai was mentally figuring out their escape route. 'We should get ourselves outside first,' he replied. 'Then we rescue her by breaking open the station wall.'

'I'm not leaving her alone underground.'

'Mole is with her,' said Sarema. 'She is as safe as she can be, for he knows the underground passages better than anyone.'

'Look where the rats are coming from,' said Kai. 'If we take the tunnel towards Langsdaine, we'll be in their path.'

'Then so will my sister!'

'No she won't. She's up against the station wall and

shut off from the tunnel. The rats aren't coming in from outside. They're running from where the explosions took place, which is much nearer here.'

'Yet . . .' Sarema paused.

'What?' asked Kai. 'What are you thinking?'

'That the only time I've seen rats flee in large numbers is when water is involved.'

'No matter what the cause is we should do the evacuation,' said Leo. 'We can step down from here onto the chairs and move them along as we go.'

They clambered from the Cage to join the others.

'The rats are nearly gone.' Cautiously Tech lowered himself to the floor. 'I'll switch the main lights back on.'

'And then we can get out by our emergency exit routes,' said Raven.

'We should wait for Spartacus to return with the rest of the money,' said Boudicca.

'Yeah,' said Beowulf. 'I agree with Boudicca.'

'The fuses in the main lighting panel have been tampered with,' Tech called out. 'I'll put on my backup system to give us some emergency lighting.'

'Who would have done that?' asked Bird Girl.

The Cage Fighters looked at each other.

'None of us,' said Sarema. 'We were all watching the fight.'

'Spartacus must have done it,' said Tech. 'Apart from me he's the only person who knew where the lighting panel was.'

'But why?' Leo's voice had a catch in it. 'Why would Spartacus do that? He's got a share in this project same as the rest of us.'

'Maybe he's changed his mind about "sharing" . . .' Tech faltered over the last word.

'You mean he was only in it to make money for himself?' Kai's voice registered his overwhelming shock as his dreams and hopes shrank by the second. 'Spartacus has betrayed us?'

Someone slipped their hand into his. He turned his head. Bird Girl was beside him.

'We need to get to the storeroom,' said Magog. 'That's where the safe with the money is. I say we split the cash there between us.'

'Sounds like a good idea to me.' Boudicca jumped from her chair and sent a couple of rats flying with the toe of her boot.

Kai glanced down. There were far fewer rats, mainly older, slower ones scuttling at the end of the trail. The floor was almost clear to walk upon.

With the rest following him, Magog strode out of the Arena to the storeroom. He forced his shoulder against the door. But the door was solid and the lock firm.

Bird Girl was hopping from foot to foot in agitation. 'I'm off,' she said. 'I think I can remember the way I came in.'

'I know you tried to memorize the route, but you might get lost,' said Kai, 'or meet Spartacus.'

Beowulf and Leo were helping Magog, taking turns at trying to force the door lock. Boudicca and Medusa were busy bringing everyone's rucksacks from their dens.

'Gita and I will also leave now,' said Sarema. 'There is great danger in remaining here.'

Kai saw that they weren't prepared to hang on. He wanted to go with them. But he wanted his money. He *needed* his money. The lock was still resisting the blows from Magog.

'I'm going.' Tech closed down his film camera and handed it to Raven, who stuffed it in the shoulder bag.

'Me too,' she said. 'That door will take ages to smash through. I'm not risking getting caught by the police.'

'But our money's in there!' Boudicca wailed, dropping the rucksacks behind them. She paused. 'We need to work out where we can meet up topside because Spartacus will come down here and get it for us later. Won't he . . . ?'

Kai hovered, undecided. The scratches on his neck were aching and he was beginning to feel dizzy. Raven and Tech picked up their rucksacks.

'Wait,' said Kai. 'I'll come with you.'

At that moment the door of the storeroom opened.

From the inside.

A young teenage girl stood in the entrance.

CHAPTER
THIRTY-ONE

'Darcey!'

Bird Girl rushed to hug her sister.

'Shhh!' Darcey said severely. She opened up her hands which were clasped to her chest and showed a bird's nest with three fledglings nestled in it.

'How did you get here?'

Darcey glanced about her, confused as to where she was.

'Is Mole OK?' Bird Girl asked her.

'Yes,' Darcey replied. 'He's with Albert. Albert knows how to be safe.'

'Was it Mole who brought you—' Bird Girl was cut off by the gabble as the Cage Fighters thronged into the room.

And it was immediately plain there would be no money for anyone. The door of the safe was ajar – and it was empty!

'Still think Spartacus is going to return?' Raven asked Boudicca.

Boudicca shouldered her rucksack. 'I'm going then, before the police arrive.' Her voice was cracking, her upset obvious.

Beowulf searched among packages and crates, but there was nothing of value to be had, and no trace even of the box containing their mobile phones. Shouting and swearing Leo began to hurl items from the shelves onto the floor. Sarema stepped in to speak to him, talking quietly until he calmed himself.

'I think we should move out as quickly as possible,' said Kai. 'The noise of that explosion might have been picked up outside and reported to the police.'

It was Tech who brought them together. He dressed Kai's wounds and checked they had snacks and water bottles before discussing an exit plan.

'If we ever want to meet up we can contact each other via the gym,' he said. He gave a wry smile. 'You never know. Maybe Spartacus is waiting there for us with all the money intact.'

Nobody smiled in response.

'Gutted.' One word from Magog summed up the general feeling.

The rehearsed evacuation allowed for four groups, each taking a different route: north, south, east and west. East was where Mole had been working on the caved-in roof which might still be unstable. The school exit lay south but they reckoned it was best not to go in the direction the rats had run.

'North or west then?' asked Tech.

'South,' said a voice no one recognized.

'Darcey?' Bird Girl turned to her sister. 'What makes you say south?'

'Albert said to go south.' Darcey raised her head, then lowered it again to focus her attention on the chicks she held.

Bird Girl glanced at Kai. Kai looked at Raven. She turned to Tech.

'Are you thinking that north via the green Main Tunnel is best?' Tech asked them. 'I'll come with you.'

'Us too,' Sarema said, holding tight onto Gita's hand.

Kai and Raven were for it. It was their emergency evacuation line and the shortest exit route. Bird Girl agreed – it made sense to go that way rather than listen to Darcey, who was probably quite confused.

'I'm heading west,' said Boudicca. 'That's my emergency exit and I'm not taking advice from a rat to go after other rats. Better we split up anyway. We'll move faster and attract less attention when we surface.'

Medusa, Beowulf and Magog agreed to go with her.

'What about you?' Boudicca asked Leo.

Leo hesitated and then shook his head. 'I'll go with Raven,' he said.

'Your loss,' said Boudicca and, with the briefest of

goodbyes, her group marched off west on the Main Tunnel.

Tech gave Bird Girl the spare torch he kept in his camera bag. He took his own from his rucksack and waited for the others to do the same. 'Want me to lead the way?' he asked them.

Nobody argued. Although Tech had never thoroughly explored the tunnels he'd set up the cameras and oversaw the monitors. 'Kai, will you bring up the rear?'

Kai nodded. Raven moved up to the front with Tech, closely followed by Leo. Sarema and Gita were sandwiched between. Darcey clutched the nest in one hand while Bird Girl took her sister's other hand. They came beside Kai at the end of the line.

As they entered the tunnel Kai looked back at the place that had been his home for the last two months. It looked desolate in the harsh light, with the café and Arena empty, parts of their costumes discarded, and debris from the storeroom strewn around. But still . . . for those short weeks of his life he'd felt safe there. And now he was going into the darkness, to nothing and with nothing.

They'd hardly gone five metres when Raven said: 'Anyone notice anything different?'

'Like what?' Tech stopped walking.

'Dunno.' Raven gave her head a little shake. 'Just . . . different.'

There was a silence. Then Sarema said, 'I can't hear anything.'

'Me neither,' said Leo.

'Kai?' Raven called back to him. 'We've been in this tunnel a few times. You think anything's off-key?'

'Uhhh . . .' It was unnaturally silent. Hairs rose on the back of Kai's neck. Crawling into his mind was the suspicion that someone *could* be watching. And you'd not know. Never know. Until it was too late.

'That's good then, isn't it?' said Bird Girl. 'That there's nothing to hear?'

'Mole says that there's always *something* to hear.' Kai spoke slowly. The earth being alive, the stones themselves organic. Kai wondered if perhaps Mole saw spirits: ghosts of those who died during the Blitz. But he knew he mustn't spook the others. 'It's OK,' he said. 'Keep walking.'

But in another metre or so something did go wrong that they couldn't help but notice. One by one their torches faded and went out. The only one left shining was the torch carried by Bird Girl. They stopped while Tech looked at the batteries.

'These are not new batteries. Someone's replaced them with used ones.'

'Spartacus?' asked Bird Girl.

'But why would he do that?' asked Leo.

'To slow us down,' Tech answered.

'Or make us return to HQ where the lights are on,' suggested Sarema.

'He wants to keep us there!' Raven voiced their fears aloud.

'Bird Girl is carrying my own torch that I brought underground and kept in my camera bag,' Tech said in an encouraging voice. 'I'll use it.'

'We'll get lost.' Bird Girl's voice resonated with apprehension.

'Raven and I know this route.' Kai tried to copy Tech's positive attitude. 'And I always counted the steps between direction changes. I can do that if everyone keeps quiet.'

Kai made his best estimate as to how many steps they'd already taken. Ten short of his total, Tech's torch illuminated the slash of blue on the wall next to Access Chute 4.

They squirmed in and climbed down the ladder.

What had taken him and Raven less than a minute seemed to take an age for eight people plus Darcey, who was making sure the birds' nest was snuggled against her chest.

Now they were on the lower level, alongside the floodwater runoff from one of the small underground rivers.

In the wavering light of one torch they lurched forwards. Water was spilling from the overflow gulleys at each side. The slapping sound echoed eerily from the walls as it burbled and gurgled along.

They approached the bend before Air Duct 6 and, even before Tech's warning cry, Kai knew that they were in trouble.

Real trouble.

At first he thought the growing noise was the sound of traffic and the disturbance around his legs a few stray rats. When he felt something slosh over his shoes he stooped and touched them. Liquid was swirling around his ankles.

Moving fast and rising.

And then a wall of water came roaring round the corner, throwing Tech and Raven aside, battering Leo and Bird Girl against the wall and knocking Darcey right off her feet.

CHAPTER
THIRTY-TWO

Kai snatched at Darcey as she went down. His fingers connected with her hair. He gathered a huge handful and hauled her clear.

Spluttering and coughing Darcey's only concern was the birds. She held her hands above her head, fingers curved around the birds' nest.

'Darcey! Let the nest go!' Bird Girl entreated her sister as she realized what she was doing. 'You need both hands to keep your balance!'

For answer Darcey raised her hands higher, still gripping the nest.

'Back up!' Tech was screaming. 'There's more water on the way! Back up!'

'Get rid of your rucksacks and join hands!' Kai shouted. He shed his own rucksack as he felt the swell of the next wave buckle his knees, staggering as the backflow swamped his waist.

A ray of light arced in the air, reflecting on the water, letting Kai see how high the level had risen. Then they were plunged into utter darkness.

'Kai!' Sarema called out. 'Kai? Are you there? Tech's torch is gone. We can't find it.'

'Forget the torch!' Kai shouted. 'Link up!'

Keeping a grip on Darcey's hair Kai reached for Bird Girl. Their fingers connected . . . and separated as another eddy of water surged between them. Where had she gone? He could hear splashing, someone moaning. Was that Gita?

Tech was doing a roll call of their names. Everyone answered.

Apart from Bird Girl.

Kai's heart was hammering in his chest. 'Bird Girl?' With his free hand he paddled the surface, slashing in the widest circle he could. 'Bird Girl!' His voice came out a croak. She'd been swept away!

Then a figure broke surface beside him, choking and gagging.

'Got you!' Kai said. He bent to tighten his arm around her waist and, pushing Darcey ahead of him, waded back to the access chute.

Without the rucksacks and driven by fear they climbed up faster than they'd come down.

Too fast.

A dozen or so steps up and Kai's shoe soles, slimy with filthy water, slipped. Darcey slid with him. He crashed onto Bird Girl, bumping them both down a rung, two . . . three . . . recovered himself, and managed to stop.

'Sorry! Sorry!' he gasped as he heard the commotion and cries of fear. Hanging on grimly, he reconnected his feet with the ladder and began again.

One step and another.

And another.

'The nest!' Darcey screeched from above his head. 'I've dropped it! It'll fall into the water! The chicks will die.' And her shoes were on his head and then his shoulders as she tried to squeeze past Kai back down the chute.

Tech was bawling. 'Keep moving! The level's rising! The current's faster. Hurry! It will pull us down like a whirlpool.'

Darcey was straining and sobbing and pushing against Kai. His fingers began to lose their grip on the rung. He was going to fall, cannon into those below him and, this time, take them to the bottom. To where the churning flood water would drag them under with its deadly power.

There was a scuffle and then Leo, who'd slithered over Tech's shoulders shouted, 'I've got it! I've got the nest!' and scooped up the nest as it hit the water.

'Come on.' Kai put his mouth close to Darcey's ear. 'If

you want to see those chicks fly you have to climb up the ladder.'

'Have you got the nest?' She snuffled the question.

'Leo's got it and . . .' Kai hesitated. 'Leo's a great guy and he'll look after it for you until we get to the top.'

Arms aching with propelling Darcey ahead of him, Kai reached out constantly with his left hand, groping for his marker stone. Exhaustion crept up on him. Blood was seeping through the dressing Tech had put on his fight wounds and trickling down his neck. He was exhausted. They should be there by now. Had he missed it? Would they climb onwards and upwards and become hopelessly lost? With no light to guide them they could wander for ever in these passageways and never be found.

Kai shut off these thoughts and tried to reason logically. It was taking longer because they were moving more slowly.

Raven's voice came echoing. 'Kai! Watch out for our junction opening!'

Maybe he'd passed the opening without knowing. Distance was hard to judge in complete darkness. He should have counted the number of rungs on the ladder.

Raven's voice again. 'Kai. I counted my steps too. You must be almost there.'

Kai stretched out his left hand. There was a space. He smoothed his hand over the surface. A craggy piece of stone! Tears ran down his cheeks as his fingers connected with the lump of protruding rock where the chute met the green Main Tunnel.

They sat huddled close to each other. Teeth chattering, shaking with reaction to the trauma and the cold, conscious of the noise of the water lapping at the bottom of the chute.

'Thank you, Leo,' Darcey said as he found her and gave her the birds' nest. 'You are very brave.'

'What do we do now?' Bird Girl whispered in the blackness.

'Back to HQ,' said Tech. 'This green line tunnel slopes upward so we're safer there.'

'And then?' asked Raven.

'Albert said to go south,' said Darcey.

'Of course he did,' said Bird Girl, soothing her.

'And south is where we should have gone,' said Sarema.

'With the rats?' Kai asked.

'The rats were going away from the flood water, running to safety.' Sarema heaved a sigh. 'We should have realized that and followed them. We didn't pay enough attention when Darcey said Albert told her which direction to take. It wasn't Albert who was telling Darcey the safest route. It was Mole. He must have found out what Spartacus intended, dug through the fallen rock and brought Darcey to the storeroom with the message to go south.'

'Of course!' said Tech. 'South is the exit with the

incline leading to the ladder which is well above river level.'

'Kai, can you find the way to HQ in the dark?' Bird Girl was very close to him.

'We'll do it together,' said Kai.

They saw the lights shining out from HQ before they heard the noise.

On seeing the glow at the end of the tunnel they automatically increased their pace. And then stopped, colliding with each other, as a sound reached their ears. A sound they'd never heard underground before.

'I like dogs.' Darcey detached herself from Bird Girl and went forward to greet the Alsatians and their police handlers. 'Not as much as birds,' she added. 'But I do like dogs a lot.'

CHAPTER
THIRTY-THREE

'Yes,' the detective answered Raven's question. 'You were betrayed.'

'Spartacus?'

'If that's what you call the man who set the explosives which blocked your exits and burst an underground river channel causing some of the tunnels to flood, then yes. But I don't think his intention was to harm you, just to keep you contained while he fiddled the bank accounts and got away. I'm guessing he was the one who made the phone call to give us the location of the HQ of the *Cage Fighters for Freedom* and tell us we'd have to dig you out – and that there was a girl trapped inside the old Langsdaine Station.'

'Did you catch him?' Bird Girl asked.

'We'll call it a work in progress,' replied the detective. 'But even without his phone call we were closing in. You were betrayed in another way.'

Leo pointed at Bird Girl. 'It was her, wasn't it?'

'No,' said the policeman. 'It was you.'

'Leo!' said Kai. 'You weasel!'

'That's rubbish!' Leo's face turned the colour of putty. 'Why would I do that? I've the most to lose.'

'To be fair,' the detective replied, 'Leo didn't know he was doing it.'

'No?' said Kai. 'How does that work?'

'Because, technically, it was her.' The detective turned his attention to Raven.

'Liar!' Raven was on her feet.

Tech grasped her hand. 'They're trying to get information from us while they wait for more officers to take us topside. He's messing with you.'

'I'm not,' said the detective. 'I'm sympathetic to your situation. From what I can gather you've worked really hard on your scheme, both for money and a worthy cause. This man Spartacus fooled you into thinking there'd be rewards for you at the end. Instead he's siphoned your money off into a phoney account. But the Fraud Squad are on the case, and it can be simple things that catch a criminal out. Al Capone, the infamous American Mob gangster, was eventually done for income tax fraud. Did you know that?'

'It was actually Kai, wasn't it?' said Leo. 'Him chasing after Bird Girl that day. You saw them on the street CCTV and it was easy to link them to the park and wonder about his sudden appearance – coming out of the gate without first going in.'

'I, like your nail varnish.' The detective took Leo's hand and inspected the fingers. 'It's not an ordinary shade of orange, is it? To match your image you wear Fluorescent Wild-Orange. We'd been watching the film clips of your fights. Initially *Cage Fighters for Freedom* was thought to be an illegal gambling scam, but after a while we began to worry it was something bigger. Your leader covered his trail expertly when posting the fights online so we couldn't track the server or the source. But a sharp-eyed police officer noticed that you always wore the same orange nail varnish: so distinctive that they found out exactly what shade it was. And there's only one which is that unique colour. One evening, on her way into the tunnels, Raven made a detour to pick some up.'

'You stole the nail varnish!' said Boudicca. 'Spartacus warned against shoplifting!'

'I *didn't* shoplift!' Raven shouted. 'I'm not that stupid!'

'Raven didn't steal the bottles of nail varnish,' said the detective. 'The manufacturer was contacted and we asked them to reduce the number of outlets they supplied. We ensured that the CCTV cameras were working properly, not only in those stores but in the streets round about. Thereafter it was a waiting and watching game. The moment that barcode went through a till we had you.'

Kai groaned. 'It would have been better if Raven had been a thief. But Spartacus said if we got done for shoplifting it would ruin the whole project.'

'I can't believe you were able to follow Raven,' said Tech. 'She's so alert.'

'No one personally followed her. It took us time to track her movements using the street CCTV. And even longer to work out the point where she disappeared from view. After that it was a case of getting the London Underground involved and studying the old maps to find out where you were.'

'If only everyone had kept to the List of Rules,' Kai said bitterly.

> Do nothing unusual.
> Do nothing out of the ordinary.
> Do nothing that attracts attention to yourself.

'I'm sorry,' said Leo. 'I'm sorry, sorry, sorry.'

Sweet revenge, thought Kai. He turned to enjoy mocking Leo for the vanity that had helped the police trace the Cage Fighters.

Leo put his head in his hands. 'It's my fault,' he sobbed. 'It's all my fault. I betrayed everyone.'

'Leo, what you did wasn't betrayal.' Sarema went over to him. 'Betrayal is when a person gives another person away deliberately.'

'I'm responsible for everyone being caught by the police.'

'Then you are also responsible that we are all safe,' said Sarema. 'For if the police had not arrived with their rescue equipment, then perhaps some of us would not be alive.'

That's not one hundred per cent true, Kai thought. Both groups of Cage Fighters had made it back to HQ, and it remained free of water. But then he recalled Leo rescuing the baby chicks, and he clamped his mouth shut.

'There's enough food and water here to keep you going.' The detective glanced around the storeroom. 'I'm going to check if the exits have been secured before I move you to the surface. There will be officers guarding the door until then.'

'I'm quite glad we've been caught.' Beowulf was the first to speak when the policeman left. 'I reckon we'll get a load of media attention when this story breaks. Maybe we can make some cash from that.'

'Trending on Twitter?' asked Magog.

'It's possible,' said Tech. 'I saved the film of the last match and I'll make sure it gets out there. Not merely the fight but the message behind the project. I don't know about you guys, but I was proud of our *Cage Fighters for Freedom*. It seemed to sum up the life of street kids – fighting to break free but caged by multi-nationals, bad government legislation, incompetence and uncaring officials.'

'Internet advertising could bring money in too then,' said Beowulf.

'But you lost the camera bag in the flood,' Medusa said sadly.

'Yeah, but not the file.' Raven lowered her voice and pointed to the thick plait of hair wound round her head. She looked at Bird Girl. 'It's not the first memory card I've kept hidden.'

'Why did you do that for me?' Bird Girl asked her. 'Stop Spartacus from getting hold of my camera card?'

'I was brought up in children's homes, like you and Dove were. Nobody wanted to adopt me either. Kind of admired you for sticking with your sister through those years.'

'I'm just thinking,' said Kai. 'If Mole brought Dove into the storeroom without unlocking the door then there must be a secret way in and out of here.'

'Darcey.' Bird Girl took her sister by the hand. 'How did Mole bring you into this room?'

Darcey shook her head. 'I promised not to tell,' she said.

'A rat!' Magog pointed. 'Sitting on that crate by the wall! Throw me a tin and I'll kill it.'

'No!' shouted Darcey. 'It's Albert! Don't kill him! It's Mole's rat. It's Albert!'

CHAPTER
THIRTY-FOUR

The crate shifted to reveal Mole.

'How did you get here?' Bird Girl asked him.

Kai recalled the conversation between Mole and Spartacus in Tech's den and he answered the question: 'Mole don't need no key to get into any storeroom.'

Mole grinned in response. 'Don't need no key to get *out* of a storeroom neither.' He pointed behind the crate. 'There be loose bricks there. Air-vent shaft. Can take you topside if'n you do so want.'

'Can you take me back to where I was before?' said Darcey.

Mole shook his head and Kai could have sworn there were tears in his eyes. 'Baby birds do need to fly outside.'

'Mole's right.' Bird Girl spoke to her sister. 'The chicks would die if you kept them underground. We must go to the surface and let them be free to live in the open air.'

'But, but, will I ever see Albert again?' Darcey asked Mole.

'Come a day you be a-standin' in Tube station waitin' for a train. An' ye'll see a white rat a little ways along the line. That'll be Albert poppin' up to say hello.'

'Really? Is that a promise?' Darcey didn't take her eyes off Mole's face.

'Lick 'n' spit,' said Mole. 'Cross my heart and hope to die.'

'I'm not leaving this area either,' said Leo. 'I need to get a custodial sentence over with.'

'Custody? Leo?' said Kai. 'I thought it was a hospital your parents wanted to put you in?'

'The story Leo told us isn't quite correct,' said Sarema. 'Would you like me to explain?' she asked him.

Leo nodded and turned his face to the wall.

'Leo wasn't being bullied at school,' said Sarema. 'Leo *was* the bully. He didn't have his arm broken. It was he who inflicted injury on a classmate. As it had happened before, he was due to be sent to a locked institution, so he ran away. But' – she took Leo's hand – 'we've been talking, and Leo's decided to try to make amends.

'Gita and I will also remain and speak to the detective,' Sarema went on. 'We've decided to ask for help from a women's refuge.'

'Raven?' said Kai. 'You coming?'

Raven shook her head.

'But you said that if you were picked up by the police,

they'd send you back to the hostel with the creepy warden.'

'Spartacus made me believe that's what would happen, but I'm going to make sure the warden of that hostel is charged.'

'You told me you weren't strong enough to cope with that. You couldn't do it on your own.'

'She won't be on her own,' said Tech. 'Raven will be with me.'

'With *you*?'

'Yeah. Me.' Tech reached out and brushed Raven's hand with his fingertips.

Kai had seen that gesture before. In Tech's den when Raven handed him the SD card from Bird Girl's camera. He thought about the looks they'd exchanged, Tech saying he'd given Raven his towel to dry her hair the day they'd captured Bird Girl. Plus a dozen other little connections. Suddenly it all added up. And Kai understood the reason Raven hung around when Tech was editing.

'I'll look after her.'

'Each other,' said Raven. 'We'll look out for each other.'

'But Tech, you'll get done for filming something illegal.'

'I doubt it,' said Tech. 'I reckon there's not much they can charge us with. And you could claim that we're the victims here.'

'All that work for nothing.'

'I don't see it that way,' said Tech. 'I've done what I set out to do. Make a film memorial for my young sister who died on the street. I intend to tackle social justice issues.' He glanced at Raven. 'One case in particular to start with.'

'If Tech reckons we can earn from the film and his media promotion then I'm staying too,' said Boudicca. 'Anyone else?'

Everyone except Kai agreed. He looked at Bird Girl. She raised her hand in farewell. 'Hope to see you sometime,' she said.

Kai hesitated.

'You go, Kai,' said Sarema. 'You wanted to travel, so that's what you should do. Find somewhere to hide out for long enough to grow a beard and then take off. Be happy.'

Gita produced a snack bar from beneath her shawl.

Kai took it and, touching his forehead, he saluted her, and all of them.

Then he climbed into the gap in the wall.

CHAPTER
THIRTY-FIVE

Kai stayed in the skip for over a week before he decided to move on.

His hair and chin stubble had grown enough to change his looks and the weather had improved so it would be easier to hitch lifts on the open road. One morning he was gathering his gear in plastic carrier bags when there was a grating noise from outside. It wasn't made by a cat or dog or any wild animal. Someone had climbed into the skip and slid down the chute.

Kai was trapped. His worst fear had happened. He wanted to barge past whoever it was and make a run for freedom, but a wave of sickness swept up from his stomach, rooting him to the ground.

The hut door opened and Bird Girl stood there.

'Hi,' she said.

Kai glanced towards the top of the skip. 'Are the police or the Social with you?'

'No.' Bird Girl shook her head. 'But I wouldn't hang about here too long if I were you. In case you haven't heard, they've arrested Spartacus. He might tell them everything and anything in order to cut some kind of deal. And I'm not sure that I fooled him that first time we met when I said that the inside of the skip was disgusting.'

'You didn't,' said Kai. 'Spartacus sussed that I'd made it into a bolt-hole. But he must have cared for me a bit because he warned me not to come back here. Said that as soon as one other person knew about a secret place then it was no longer safe, or secret . . .' Kai tilted his head. 'I guess it depends on the person.'

'I guess so.' Bird Girl met his eyes.

'Why *did* you agree with Spartacus when he said that the skip was filthy inside?'

'It seemed the right thing to do.' She paused. 'I got the feeling that it was your private place and you wouldn't be happy for anyone to know about it.'

'Thanks,' said Kai.

She looked at his carrier bags. 'Were you about ready to leave?' she asked him.

'I'm going away,' said Kai. 'For a while anyway,' he added. 'To clear my head.'

'I thought you might need this.' Bird Girl handed him

a rucksack. 'And . . . there's something in it that belongs to you.'

Kai opened it up and saw a box.

A shoe box.

Hands shaking Kai lifted it out. Inside was his model of Treasure Island.

'The underground *Cage Fighters for Freedom* are hot news,' said Bird Girl. 'It's all over the media, with details of their families if they've got any. I was able to find out where your mum lived and I went to see her to tell her you were OK. She gave me that in case I ever met up with you. Says she found it under your bed the day before you left and realized something was very wrong. She took it away to fix it before she spoke to you about it. Eddy tried to explain why it was smashed – gave her a whole story about your fits of bad temper. But she knew that this was the one model you'd never break, no matter what teenage strop you were in. She said she tried to mend it, but that she was never as good as you with the intricate parts.'

Kai felt tears itching at the back of his eyes. With trembling fingers, he picked up the tiny treasure chest that sat under the broken palm trees.

'Your mum also said that Eddy has moved out. Says she can live her life without having him around any more.'

'She'll never need to rely on anyone ever again.' Kai took some coins from his pocket. 'Could you sell these discreetly and give her the money from me?'

Bird Girl's mouth rounded in astonishment as she looked at the coins. 'These are gold sovereigns! Where did you get them?'

'Mole gave them to me,' said Kai. And he told her how, when they reached an exit from underground, he'd tried to persuade Mole to leave the tunnels.

'Mole,' Kai had said, 'won't you come to the surface with me?'

'Can't do that.'

'Why not?'

'I'd be like them pit ponies. Grampa told me. A hundred years ago. Be put down mine to work. When they be taken topside, they do go blind.'

'I'd get you a pair of sunglasses. Designer shades,' Kai tried to joke. 'You'd look cool.'

Mole shook his head. 'I do like to dig. Don't know nothin' else to do.'

'Listen, Mole.' Kai spoke carefully so as not to upset his friend. 'I don't think you're ever going to find your grampa's gold.'

'I do have the gold already.' Mole pulled a filthy rag from his trouser pocket and unfolded it. A heap of sovereigns gleamed burnished yellow.

'You found the gold!'

'I do discover it long ago.'

'Mole!' Kai gasped.

'For you.' Mole thrust the coins at Kai. 'I got plenty more.'

'Are you sure you won't come with me?' Kai asked him.

'I die up there,' Mole whispered. 'I be safe here. I do go where nobody find me.' And saying that, he scooped Albert into his pocket and disappeared into the darkness.

Kai had no idea how much the coins were worth, but even selling one or two in a dodgy shop should give him a decent amount of money.

'You mustn't mention the coins to anyone,' he told Bird Girl. 'Not even my mum.'

'I won't,' she assured him. 'And I'll suggest she doesn't let Eddy find out that she's got some ready cash in the house. He's trying to win her back by attending an anger management programme and he's promised to stop drinking.'

'He'll not do it,' said Kai. 'He'll pretend he has, but he won't.'

'Well, he's admitted he was very jealous of you and your relationship with your mum. Eddy couldn't understand that your mum could love you and him at the same time.' Bird Girl paused. 'It's hard to work through emotions. But I think it is possible to love more than one person. I love my sister, Darcey, but that doesn't mean' – she stole a glance at Kai – 'that I couldn't also fall in love with someone.'

'I'm not going home,' said Kai. 'Well, not yet, anyway.'

'Your mum said she thought you might want to travel a bit.'

'That's what I'm going to do,' said Kai.

'I've got something else for you,' Bird Girl said briskly. She gave Kai a packet swaddled in a scarf. 'Gita sent some snack bars and Sarema wrapped them up in one of her scarves.'

Kai placed the shoe box and the scarf inside the rucksack. 'I'd better pack the rest of my stuff and get started.'

'I hope you make it to your own special island.'

'I will,' said Kai. 'For sure.'

'Send me a postcard?'

'I'll do better than that.' Kai smiled. 'I'll let you know when I reach the island where the geese land when they migrate. Then you and Darcey can visit me.'

'I'll find you,' Bird Girl whispered. 'I'm good at finding people.'

She came closer to him. Her blonde hair was like golden rain around her face, and around his too, as she leaned in for his kiss.

If you enjoyed *Caged*, why not try these other titles by Theresa Breslin?

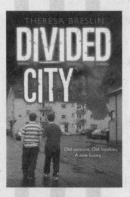

DIVIDED CITY
'A skilfully-plotted
page-turner'
INIS

GHOST SOLDIER
'This is a cracking
good book'
*Guardian Children's
Books*

KEZZIE AT WAR
'A touching story...
Vividly described'
*Times Educational
Supplement*

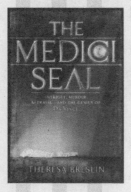

THE MEDICI SEAL
'A richly drawn and
fascinating look at
16th-century Italy'
The Bookseller

**THE NOSTRADAMUS
PROPHECY**
'A superb and totally
gripping story'
The School Librarian

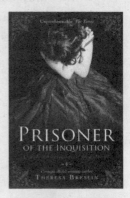

**PRISONER OF THE
INQUISITION**
'Very gripping, and
difficult to put down'
BCF Book Reviews